THE GOLDEN COMPASS™

THE OFFICIAL ILLUSTRATED
MOVIE COMPANION

BRIAN SIBLEY

SCHOLASTIC

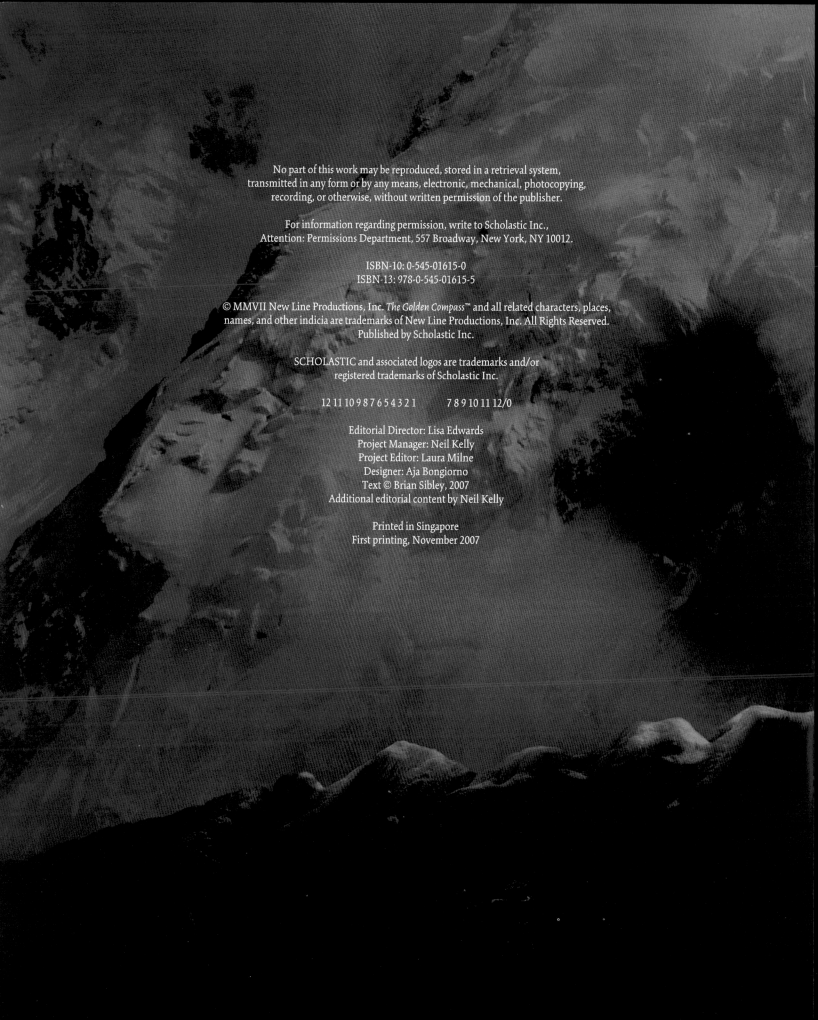

For information regarding permission, write to Scholastic Inc.,
Attention: Permissions Department, 557 Broadway, New York, NY 10012.

ISBN-10: 0-545-01615-0
ISBN-13: 978-0-545-01615-5

12 11 10 9 8 7 6 5 4 3 2 1   7 8 9 10 11 12/0

Editorial Director: Lisa Edwards
Project Manager: Neil Kelly
Project Editor: Laura Milne
Designer: Aja Bongiorno
Text © Brian Sibley, 2007
Additional editorial content by Neil Kelly

Printed in Singapore
First printing, November 2007

CONTENTS

INTRODUCTION

"When my mother first read Philip Pullman's books to me," remembers Dakota Blue Richards, "I couldn't get a face for Lyra in my head, so I pictured her as me — that's all I had to imagine her with...."

Like many children all over the world, 12-year-old British actress Dakota was a huge fan of *The Golden Compass*, the classic children's fantasy novel written by renowned author Philip Pullman. The book's feisty heroine, Lyra Belacqua, has become one of the best-loved heroines of children's literature. But Dakota — unlike the millions of other children who have thrilled to Lyra's adventures — was lucky enough to have the amazing experience of becoming the character, in Scholastic Media and New Line Cinema's spectacular new movie adaptation of *The Golden Compass*.

The first book in the best-selling *His Dark Materials* trilogy, *The Golden Compass* is a spellbinding novel set in an amazing parallel universe. It tells the story of Lyra, a willful young orphan who embarks on an epic quest to the frozen North of her world. On her travels she encounters beautiful and ageless witches, daringly heroic Gyptians, and fearsome armored Ice Bears.

The journey from novel to screen has been many years in the making. The original book was never fully illustrated, so, like Dakota, readers have had to imagine the fascinating characters and settings for themselves. But for those who come to the story of *The Golden Compass* for the first time through the film, the on-screen realization of Philip Pullman's novel will become the definitive visualization of Lyra's world.

The Golden Compass: The Official Illustrated Movie Companion reveals the story behind the making of the movie. From the origins of the screenplay through to the stunning production design, inspired casting, fantastic costumes, and dazzling visual effects, this book celebrates the creative talent of the team behind one of the most ambitious motion pictures of all time.

So read on — the Compass will show you the way....

Brian Sibley, October 2007

DARKNESS INTO LIGHT

The Origins of *The Golden Compass*

On February 6, 2002, a headline in the British newspaper *The Independent* reported: "Children's author Pullman signs up with *The Lord of the Rings* team." This statement marked the fact that New Line Cinema — the Hollywood studio that produced *The Lord of the Rings* motion picture trilogy — had formed a production partnership with Scholastic Media (see page 15) to film *His Dark Materials*, an award-winning series of novels popular with young readers and much praised by literary critics.

> "Education should be about lighting a fire in the child's mind, filling it with desire and delight and curiosity...."
>
> PHILIP PULLMAN

Pullman intended *The Golden Compass* to be the first book in a series that was inspired by *Paradise Lost*, the epic poem written by 17th-century English poet John Milton. *Paradise Lost* consists of 12 books, or sections, and tells the story of a war between Heaven and Hell. The series title for the trilogy —"*His Dark Materials*"— also has its origins in a line from the poem.

Written by best-selling British author Philip Pullman (pictured above), the first novel in the epic trilogy collectively known as *His Dark Materials* was published in 1995. Entitled *Northern Lights* in the UK (see page 11), it was subsequently released under a very different title in the United States and most of the rest of the world — *The Golden Compass*. A former schoolteacher, Pullman had written many school plays during his teaching career, some of which he decided to reinvent as novels for children. His first book for children was published in 1982, and 11 years and several successful volumes later he began writing the book that would eventually become *The Golden Compass*.

▶ *Philip Pullman provided the introduction for a special edition of Milton's Paradise Lost published by the Oxford University Press.*

JOHN MILTON
PARADISE
LOST
An illustrated edition with an introduction by
PHILIP PULLMAN

◀ The Golden Compass *is the first novel in the* His Dark Materials *trilogy. Its sequels –* The Subtle Knife *and* The Amber Spyglass *– complete the epic story of Lyra Belacqua.*

The themes of Milton's *Paradise Lost* are challenging subject matter to incorporate into a book primarily written for children, but Pullman is uncompromising in his use of ideas and words. As the author puts it: "There's fast-food language and there's caviar language." It is, however, the feelings conveyed in a book that are most important for him: "Enjoy it first," he says, "and get at the meaning afterwards."

On its publication, *The Golden Compass* was an immediate success — the book was pounced on by young readers, praised by reviewers, and named as the 1995 winner of the prestigious Carnegie Medal for Children's Literature.

One of the judges of the Carnegie competition described the novel as a book that would "set young minds on fire." In his acceptance speech, Pullman made clear his intention to challenge his readers: "There are some themes, some subjects, too large for adult fiction; they can only be dealt with adequately in a children's book...."

The story of *The Golden Compass* opens in the setting of Oxford, but it is not the English university city we know; instead, it is an Oxford that exists in another world in a parallel universe. This Oxford is the home of Lyra Belacqua, the heroine of Pullman's novel.

▼ *With its elegant towers and spires, the fictional institution of Jordan College in Lyra's Oxford was inspired by the real-world location of Exeter College.*

◄ *The world of* The Golden Compass *is similar to our own, with familiar continents and oceans. However, the peoples, countries, and creatures that inhabit it — including armored bears and flying witches — are very different.*

There are various similarities between Lyra's world and our own. For example, Lyra's home in her Oxford is the ancient institution of Jordan College — a fictional version of Exeter College in the real Oxford where author Philip Pullman was educated. Lyra travels to the principal city of her country, Brytain, which — like the capital of the British Isles — is called London. She then sets out on a long journey that eventually takes her to the northern land of Svalbard, which is also the name of a group of islands in our world, halfway between Norway and the North Pole.

The unique point about the Svalbard visited by Lyra — as opposed to the real Norwegian islands — is that it is ruled by a race of intelligent, armored bears, one of whom, Iorek Byrnison, becomes her friend and protector. Other differences between Lyra's universe and our own include the use of different forms of energy, transport, and technology to those seen in our world.

In addition, people's lives are controlled by an oppressive and dictatorial organization known as the Magisterium. The most remarkable thing about Lyra's world, however, is that every human being has a dæmon — a part of their soul that lives on the outside of their body in the form of an animal. A dæmon is a constant companion, always close by throughout a person's life.

► *In Lyra's London, majestic, hydrogen-filled airships float overhead, while Magisterial carriages powered by glowing anbaric energy race through the city's crowded streets.*

Dæmons can speak, but they are also able to communicate with their humans telepathically. A child's dæmon can change shape, assuming all the forms that a child's limitless potential inspires. As a person ages, their dæmon settles, according to their character and nature. Lyra's dæmon, Pantalaimon, takes on the appearance of all sorts of creatures, including a cat, an ermine, a mouse, a bird, and even a snake.

Philip Pullman admits to borrowing the idea of dæmons from the ancient Greek philosopher Socrates, who believed he had a divine presence within himself called a daimon that warned him against making mistakes but never told him what to do. "I suddenly realized that Lyra had a dæmon," says Pullman, "and it all grew out of that. Of course, the dæmons had to represent something important in the meaning of the story, and not be merely picturesque; otherwise they'd just get in the way. So there is a big difference between the dæmons of children and adults, because the story as a whole is about growing up, of innocence and experience."

In addition to the contrast between innocence and experience, the constant theme running through *His Dark Materials* is the eternal battle between good and evil — a struggle that is at the heart of many of the world's greatest books. Lyra gets caught up in this age-old conflict when she sets out to rescue a friend from Oxford, Roger Parslow, who has been kidnapped by a sinister group known as the Gobblers. The young heroine is helped or hindered along the way by a host of colorful characters.

The Alethiometer

Also known as the Golden Compass, the alethiometer is an extraordinarily intricate device that was made in the 16th century. But while an ordinary compass always shows true North, the alethiometer's needle points to truth itself. The ornamented face of the device is divided into 36 symbols, each of which may convey different meanings in combination with any of the others. Reading the alethiometer is a difficult task, but Lyra Belacqua possesses a natural ability to use the instrument.

▶ *Lyra Belacqua – played in* The Golden Compass *movie by Dakota Blue Richards – consults her truth-telling alethiometer.*

Northern Lights and Golden Compasses

The trilogy known as *His Dark Materials* was originally going to have a different name — *The Golden Compasses*. This title, inspired by Milton's *Paradise Lost* (see page 7), came from a line in the poem referring to the Son of God taking "the golden compasses, prepared / In God's eternal store, to circumscribe / The universe, and all created things." As Philip Pullman says, "These were compasses to draw a circle with, not a compass to find your way with." Pullman later decided that *His Dark Materials* would be a better collective title for the planned trilogy. He called the first book *Northern Lights*, in reference to the mysterious aurora that Lyra encounters at the North Pole (above). It was — and continues to be — published under this title in the UK. However, due to a misunderstanding, the editors of the U.S. edition thought that "The Golden Compasses" referred to Lyra's golden, compass-like alethiometer (see page 10). They decided that the singular version of this title — *The Golden Compass* — would be a stronger name for *Northern Lights* in the U.S. market. The title stuck, and the book is now known as *The Golden Compass* in most of the 39 languages into which it has been translated.

Lyra's uncle, Lord Asriel, is an intrepid adventurer who has made strange discoveries during his explorations to the North Pole. The elegant and alluring Mrs. Marisa Coulter is also a powerful, enigmatic figure, who — unknown to Lyra — is in some way connected with both her and Lord Asriel. Her dæmon takes the form of a beautiful but vicious Golden Monkey. Another key character is John Faa, King of the Gyptians, a race of traveling boat people, who protect Lyra and become involved in her fight to rescue Roger and other children who have been kidnapped by the Gobblers.

Lee Scoresby, a heroic aeronaut from the country of Texas, is hired by the Gyptians and uses his trusty airship to assist Lyra in her mission. Serafina Pekkala, the beautiful Clan-queen of the Witches of Lake Enara, is also enlisted in Lyra's fight against the forces of evil. Although she is several hundred years old, Serafina shows no sign of age. Like all witches, she has the power of flight.

Pullman's plucky heroine is further assisted in her quest by the use of an alethiometer, a golden device shaped like a compass. This instrument is a precious truth-telling machine, given to Lyra by the Master of Jordan College to prevent it from falling into the hands of the Magisterium.

◄ *The three books that comprise the His Dark Materials trilogy have also been published in one volume — an epic read at over 1,000 pages in length.*

► *In 1995,* The Golden Compass *was awarded the Carnegie Medal for Children's Literature.*

So the author went back into his shed to write the second novel, *The Subtle Knife*, which was published in 1997. He completed the trilogy in 2000 with the publication of the third book — *The Amber Spyglass*.

Like the first book, the sequels received rave reviews: "Philip Pullman's fictional universe blazes with vitality," read one. Another summed up the author's books in this way: "Marvels and monsters, tragedies and triumphs are unrolled with a lavishness typical of the prodigiously gifted writer."

Pullman had won the Carnegie Medal in 1995 for *The Golden Compass*, but many people were surprised when *The Amber Spyglass* won the Whitbread Book of the Year Award in 2001. In the 31 years that this major British literary prize had been awarded, it had never previously gone to a children's book. The smarter reviewers, however, pointed out that the author's writing appealed to readers of all ages.

L yra's amazing world and the memorable characters, dæmons, creatures, and inventions that inhabit it were conceived in very down-to-earth surroundings; *The Golden Compass* was famously written in a shed in the garden of Philip Pullman's former home in Oxford. Many journalists who visited Oxford to interview the author would describe the shed's wonderfully cluttered contents, such as the shelves groaning with hundreds of books (including lots of foreign-language editions of his own stories), Venetian masks, old postcards, and children's drawings. It also contained chunks of stone from different countries around the world, a guitar, a saxophone, a six-foot-high stuffed figure of a rat used in one of his stage plays, and an old computer decorated with plastic flowers.

The author himself described his shed as "a filthy, abominable pit — no one would go in there unless they absolutely had to!" However, Philip Pullman still had to complete Lyra's story.

◄ *When Philip Pullman was asked what his dæmon would be, he replied that it should be a raven because, in the mythology of North America, the raven is a trickster. "I like the idea of a storyteller being a trickster," he said, "because you are like the con man persuading people of the truth even if it is not true."*

His Dark Materials at the National Theatre

In 2003, London's Royal National Theatre staged the first major theatrical version of *His Dark Materials*. Adapted by Nicholas Wright from the novels and directed by Nicholas Hytner as a two-part, six-hour performance, it ran from December 2003 until March 2004. Starring Anna Maxwell-Martin as Lyra, Dominic Cooper as Will, Timothy Dalton as Lord Asriel, and Patricia Hodge as Mrs. Coulter, the play was a huge success. It was revived with a new cast and a revised script for a second run between November 2004 and April 2005. The production has since been staged by several UK playhouses, and has also been performed in the Republic of Ireland at the O'Reilly Theatre in Dublin, where it was staged by the dramatic society of Belvedere College.

"The author," wrote one critic, "tells an incredible story — one that will harness the imaginations of children and adults now and in future generations."

When Philip Pullman was a youngster, he had read all the books he could lay his hands on, regardless of whether they were written for children or grown-ups. As a result, he has always believed that his books are for anyone who enjoys reading them. "Down with children's books!" he once wrote. "When you say, 'This book is for children,' what you are really saying is, this book is not for grown-ups. But I don't care who's in my audience — all I care about is that there are as many of them as possible!"

Millions of readers all over the world have now taken *His Dark Materials* volumes down from the shelf and immersed themselves in the wonderful worlds they contain. At the last count, the trilogy has sold in the region of 14 million copies in 39 languages. With the release of the movie adaptation of *The Golden Compass*, many millions more, of all ages, will be introduced to Lyra Belacqua's story and will discover the remarkable books on which the movie is based.

So, let's find out how this highly successful, much-loved book written in a garden shed in Oxford became a spectacular, big-budget Hollywood movie....

▼ *For many years Philip Pullman worked in a large shed in the garden of his former house in Oxford. When he moved, he gave the shed to a friend — the illustrator Ted Dewan — on the condition that it would one day be passed on to another writer or illustrator. Pullman liked the idea that, as the shed was passed on to new owners, "each of them will replace this bit or that bit until there isn't an atom of the original shed left."*

MAKING IT HAPPEN

The Journey from Novel to Screenplay

"When I read the manuscript for *The Golden Compass* novel in 1995, I was astounded," recalls Deborah Forte (pictured below), Producer of *The Golden Compass* movie and President of Scholastic Media. "I thought Philip Pullman was such an incredible storyteller and used language in such a cinematic way that the book had to be made into a movie. I called him about making a film, and he agreed it was a good idea. And so I signed on for what turned out to be a 10-year odyssey to get *The Golden Compass* made!"

As Deborah suggests, securing the rights for Scholastic Media to get the film of *The Golden Compass* made was just the beginning of a long and difficult journey. For the next few years, she was unsure how Philip Pullman would follow up *The Golden Compass* — a book that was clearly only the beginning of what would ultimately be a much bigger, more expansive story. "Since I didn't know where Philip was going with the story, I didn't know whether, ultimately, we would be talking about one, two, or three movies. But once the third book — *The Amber Spyglass* — had been published, I started trying to get other people excited about the trilogy's film potential."

◄ *The official movie poster for* The Golden Compass *incorporates three main elements - Lyra, the alethiometer and the Ice Bear Iorek Byrnison.*

Deborah was determined to get the project made, but she was not prepared to compromise Pullman's vision. It was important that the form the adaptation took was appropriate for the material. As a result, various approaches from television were turned down while Deborah looked for a way to produce *The Golden Compass* as a big-budget, full-length feature film — potentially the first of three — made for the cinema.

However, getting the movie made would not be easy. "The reactions were exactly as you might expect," recalls Deborah. "People said, 'This would be such an expensive movie....' and 'How are you going to deal with dæmons?' And I just kept saying, 'I know, I know....' So, I just went on pitching the idea and eventually one or two people started to become interested. Then, when Philip won the Whitbread Award for *The Amber Spyglass*, more people got interested and I was able to conclude a deal with New Line Cinema."

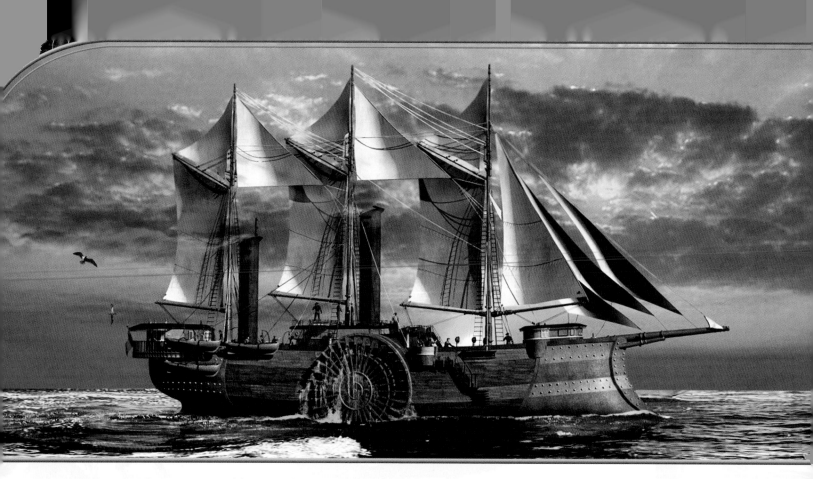

▲ *Chris Weitz, the screenwriter and director of* The Golden Compass, *sailed to the Arctic on a chartered sailing ship to provide inspiration while he wrote the screenplay. The ship on which he traveled, the* Noorderlicht, *lent its name to the fictional Gyptian ship in the movie (above).*

For New Line Cinema, fresh from its triumphs with *The Lord of the Rings* trilogy, the decision to embark upon another three-film epic may seem obvious, but it was still a daunting commitment. Nevertheless, New Line's founders, Bob Shaye and Michael Lynne, and their head of production, Toby Emmerich, instinctively responded to the project's enormous potential. "When New Line decide to back something," says Deborah, "they do it completely. They understand that to do something new and significant in film always involves risk but they are risk takers and are unafraid to pursue something in which they believe."

It is a view endorsed by the film's eventual screenwriter and director, Chris Weitz: "It was a tremendous risk for New Line Cinema to make *The Lord of the Rings*, and maybe an even bigger one with *The Golden Compass*, but through the learning process of making *The Lord of the Rings*, they became the movie studio best capable of doing this kind of film."

Chris Weitz's involvement began in the year 2000 when Chris (pictured below) and his brother, Paul Weitz, were in London directing Hugh Grant in the movie adaptation of Nick Hornby's best-selling book *About a Boy*. "Friends recommended that I read *The Golden Compass*," he remembers, "and I was immediately bowled over by it. I thought it had tremendous visual and cinematic potential, but that it was on the edge of achievability — if not beyond it — because of the sheer number of shots involving dæmons. It's one thing to have monsters or dinosaurs in a shot, but it's another thing to have the very intimate interaction between people and these creatures with essentially human emotions in every single scene."

▼ *New Line Cinema's Oscar®-winning* The Lord of the Rings *trilogy is one of the most successful film franchises in movie history.*

Founded almost 40 years ago, New Line Cinema is the most successful independent film company in the world. It produces innovative, popular motion pictures, and the studio also has divisions devoted to home entertainment, television, music, theater, and merchandising. New Line is a division of Time Warner, Inc., and in 2005 the studio partnered with HBO to form Picturehouse, a new theatrical distribution company to release independent films.

Despite these challenges, when Weitz heard that Scholastic Media and New Line Cinema were going to make the movie he pushed to become involved. "I knew the first directors they'd think of would be people like Ridley Scott, Peter Weir, and Ang Lee," says Weitz. "These are guys who've worked on large special effects projects, but who are also experienced at handling the dramatic aspects. So, I started badgering Toby Emmerich, because I figured it's in the nature of these things to come together and fall apart. I decided that I would keep on bugging people until the chance came along, and finally it did and I found myself with a job!"

Meanwhile, a first attempt had been made to come up with a screenplay. Unlike some novelists whose work is adapted for a film, Philip Pullman had no desire to write the script for *The Golden Compass* — especially after seven years of working on his trilogy. "The last thing I wanted to do," he says, "was take it all apart and put it together differently. I was happy to let someone else do it while I got on with the next book."

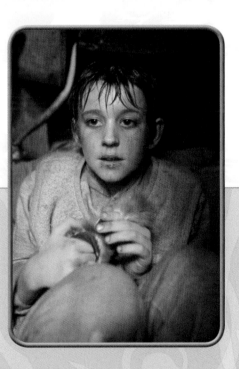

▶ *Billy Costa — played by Charlie Rowe — cowers in a remote trapper's hut in the frozen North of Lyra's world.*

Adapting the Novel

In the process of creating the screenplay for *The Golden Compass*, some of the events in Philip Pullman's original book were lost or compressed in order to fit the story into a reasonable movie running time. The characters of Billy Costa and Tony Makarios — Gyptian children kidnapped by the Gobblers — were also combined into one for the film adaptation to streamline the plot and move the action forward.

With Philip Pullman taking a step back from the screenwriting process, a script was commissioned from the highly successful British playwright and screenwriter Tom Stoppard, who had won an Oscar® for his script for the Miramax movie *Shakespeare in Love*.

Philip Pullman, who says that he doubts "whether authors ever know what their own novels mean," gave Stoppard his assistance: "He asked many questions about various aspects of the story," Pullman recalls, "questions to which often the only true answer would have been 'I don't know … I just made it up,' or 'It felt right,' or 'I just thought it needed "X" at that point.'" The resulting Stoppard script was not, in the end, what the studio was looking for and when Chris Weitz was named as the film's director, he expressed a wish to write his own screenplay. But before Chris could do that, he decided that he had to go north!

"The feeling of northerness," he explains, "and the sense of exploring on the very edge of where it is possible to survive, is central to the book. And since I've lived most of my life in comfort, I decided that if I was to have any chance of understanding Pullman's vision, I would have to go up to the Arctic. Of course, when I told Philip that I was going, he said he'd never been there!"

Chris got the last berth on a converted light-ship called the *Noorderlicht* (see page 24) and set off on his expedition, beginning with the four airplane flights required to get him from Los Angeles to Longyearbyen on Svalbard, where the ship would embark on its voyage. Once at sea, Chris settled down to begin work on his screenplay when disaster struck: "I plugged in my computer, and it blew up! There was no way of getting it repaired. I had no other choice, but sitting there, writing it the old-fashioned way with pen and paper on a ship in the Arctic, felt right!"

▼ In Lyra's world, the snowy wastes of Svalbard are dominated by the castle of King Ragnar — the leader of a race of intelligent armored Ice Bears, also known as Panserbjørne.

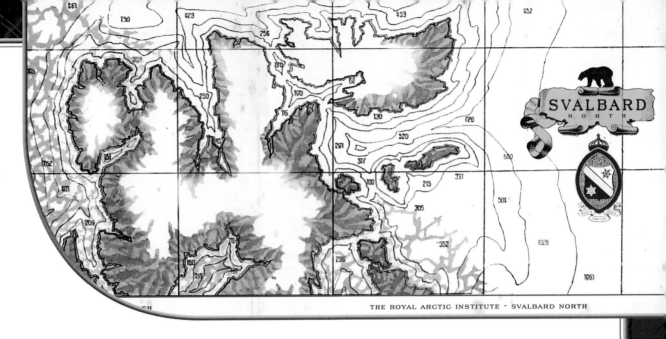

▶ Svalbard lies in the far North of Lyra's world. Many falling stars land on Svalbard, from which the Ice Bears extract tough sky-iron to forge their armor.

"The Arctic was the last place I would ever normally want to go, but I now know what it feels like to be there – which is cold, beautiful, and dangerous."

CHRIS WEITZ

Following his voyage, Chris Weitz delivered a 186-page first-draft script and then the work of editing and refining the story for the screen really began. *The Golden Compass* is an event-filled book and it was a difficult task to compress the action of the novel into the duration of a movie. "I'm not going to say it was easy to distil, a 400-page book down to a 117-page script," says Deborah Forte, "but the rule we adopted was 'stick with Lyra': It's Lyra's story and so we told the story as her journey from innocence to experience, from being this savage, lying, selfish girl who you love, to a self-sacrificing courageous young person." With the script taking shape, Deborah Forte set up a production office in London. "We really weren't sure whether we were going to get the movie green-lit, but I knew that if we did, I wanted to try to make the film in Britain because Philip Pullman and the sources of his inspiration are very British."

But then a problem arose when Chris began to doubt his ability to see the project through to completion. The daunting prospect of making a movie that featured such a vast amount of groundbreaking special effects, as well as the responsibility for handling a budget that would run to tens of millions of dollars, led to Weitz having second thoughts. While maintaining his involvement with the script, Chris relinquished the task of directing the film and another director was appointed. However, creative differences eventually led to a parting of the ways with the replacement director and, amazingly, Chris Weitz got a second chance to take on the film. "I was very lucky," he says, "and there was no chance that I was going to walk away again."

◀ Ragnar Sturlusson, the ferocious King of the Ice Bears, wears elegant, crafted armor that reflects his high status.

CLIMBING THE MOUNTAIN

Conceptualizing the World of *The Golden Compass*

When asked about his decision to walk away from directing *The Golden Compass,* Chris Weitz likened the challenge of making the movie to an attempt to climb Everest. He explains: "The thing is, you could say, 'I'd really like to climb Everest next November,' and then show up at base camp and just see this huge mountain looming up into the clouds — and start having second thoughts about it." So what was different about accepting the challenge to direct *The Golden Compass* a second time, having already turned down the job once? Surely the task still loomed like an Everest-high mountain surrounded in clouds? "Yes," says Weitz, "but there was now a team of fellow climbers to help drag me up the slope — if necessary on a stretcher!"

The first of those climbing companions was Oscar®-winning Production Designer Dennis Gassner. "People ask me what kind of a designer do I call myself," says Dennis. "I reply, 'Well, I don't know.' But I would consider myself, if anything, a 'method production designer,' because I am very involved with the characters. They are all in me. I have to understand who they are and where they've come from: I have to understand their backstory, their particular nature. Then with my set decorator, Anna Pinnock, and the rest of the design team, we spend a lot of time looking at images and talking incessantly about details." Dennis's dramatic designs have contributed to the success of such films as *Bugsy, The Truman Show, Road to Perdition, Big Fish, Waterworld,* and a string of Cohen Brothers movies, beginning with *Miller's Crossing.*

"The reason I did *The Golden Compass,*" says Gassner, "was because I felt that I could do it. As a younger designer, halfway through my career, I would have said 'No.' I wouldn't have felt that I had the experience."

◀ ▲ *Concept art developed by Dennis Gassner was used to visualize the world of* The Golden Compass. *Examples of these stunning designs include the Magisterial Sky Ferry, Mrs. Coulter's apartment, and Trollesund (all on facing page) and the Magisterial carriage (above).*

The process of conceptualizing the world of *The Golden Compass* began with the story as told in Chris Weitz's script and the book on which it was based. "You only have to read a page or so," says Dennis Gassner, "to see that Philip Pullman has an ability to seduce the reader in the finest ways. Once I'd made that discovery and understood the seduction, I said, 'He's done his job; now I have to do mine!'"

Gassner's job was to create a visual interpretation of Pullman's book, but the novel itself doesn't contain vast amounts of detailed description. So he began by finding a shorthand way of describing the film. "There are two basic elements to this story," says Dennis. "*The Golden Compass* is set in a time that we don't really know, but which we feel we know. And it's also a story of a little girl and her journey into another world beyond anything that we understand."

> *"The alethiometer gave me an image from which to begin my design — the pure image of the circle."*
>
> DENNIS GASSNER

If time is one of the two key themes of the story, maintains Dennis, then the other is power: Lord Asriel and Mrs. Coulter use and misuse earthly powers; the Witches and the Bears possess natural and supernatural powers; Lyra demonstrates the power of innocence; and the alethiometer operates by the power of truth. "Time and power," says Dennis, "are fused in the Golden Compass itself. The alethiometer gave me an image from which to begin my design — the pure image of the circle."

Once Dennis had decided on the circle as the motif used to represent the purity and innocence of Lyra, it was just a short step to decide on the motif for the power-hungry, oppressive Magisterium. "The oval," Dennis explains, "is an elongation of the pure circle: It is a circle that is trying to stretch itself and make itself bigger."

Lee Scoresby's Airship

One of the most iconic designs featured in *The Golden Compass* is Lee Scoresby's airship (left). In Pullman's novel, the vehicle is described simply as a hot-air balloon. Dennis Gassner's elegant conceptualization of the vehicle incorporates elements of sailing-ship design and features a pair of distinctive, spherical hydrogen-filled balloons to keep the vessel aloft.

▶ In The Golden Compass, Dennis Gassner uses the recurring visual theme of the oval and the circle to symbolize contrasting values. The circle, a "pure" form, represents good and/or innocence, while the oval — a distortion of the circle — represents experience, misguided ambition, and corruption. Examples of this idea seen in the movie include the following (clockwise from left to right); the alethiometer; the Magisterial emblem; the Bolvangar intercision machine; the Jordan College Retiring Room table; the wardrobe window in the Retiring Room.

▶ All of the major sets and props seen in The Golden Compass film were developed from sketches or schematics produced by Production Designer Dennis Gassner and his team. The blueprints (right) for the Noorderlicht — the oceangoing ship used by John Faa and the Gyptians — were used to build a full-scale section of the vessel for filming at Shepperton Studios in the UK. This specially constructed area is shown in the green area of the illustration.

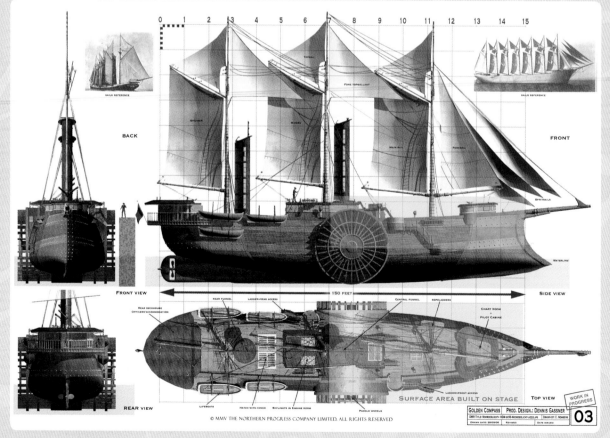

Chris Weitz had total confidence in Dennis Gassner's vision for the film: "The man is a genius and to have someone involved who was able to develop the degree of detail, the coherence of textures, and the variety of atmospheres that the film required was like having a huge piece of the jigsaw puzzle already in place." Other pieces of that puzzle quickly fell into place in the form of an award-winning lineup of creative talents. These included Ruth Myers, whose costume designs have been seen in *LA Confidential, Beyond the Sea,* and the TV series *Carnivàle,* and Peter King, who has created hair and makeup designs for, among many films, *The Lord of the Rings* trilogy, *Nanny McPhee,* and *King Kong.* The key role of Director of Photography went to Henry Braham, whose previous work includes the movies *Shooting Fish, Waking Ned,* and *Bright Young Things.* Henry received an Emmy® for his work on *Shackleton,* the acclaimed TV miniseries about the Antarctic explorer, which also gave him a valuable insight into filming in polar conditions. "When I read the script," he says, "I didn't respond to it as a fantasy film so much as an adventure movie. Of course, there are endless other layers to the story, but fundamentally it was a great adventure and a great journey."

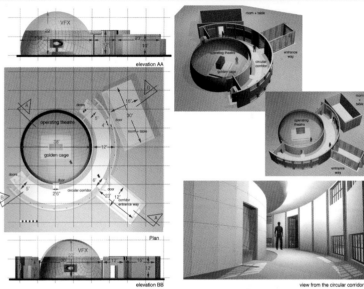

Taking on, perhaps, the biggest challenge was Visual Effects Supervisor, Mike Fink (left), whose screen credits include *X-Men* and *X-Men II, Batman Returns, Mars Attacks!, Braveheart,* and *Constantine.* "The process of trying to turn the book into a movie," says Mike Fink, "is an interesting one, because the book is a length of a novel whereas a movie is more like a short story. And I knew that when it came to the visual effects we were going to have to face exactly the same challenge. We'd have to take this immense canvas that Philip Pullman had created and include everything that needed to be there but within the running time of a film."

▲ In addition to the creation of concept art depicting key movie locations, such as the Bolvangar station (above top), detailed cutaway schematics (above middle) were also produced to enable the visual effects teams to create the three-dimensional, computer-generated imagery seen on screen (above bottom).

With all the key members of Chris Weitz's team in place and ready to scale the moviemaking mountain, the moment had finally come to see if New Line Cinema would now formally "green-light" the movie — and commit to providing the huge financial backing required to begin production.

"They threw me a challenge," Producer Deborah Forte remembers. "They said, 'Prove to us that you can do this movie!' And given the fact that this was going to be a massive financial commitment on the part of the studio, they were obviously right to do so!

So, it was up to us to prove that the script was going to work, that we could produce it for a specific amount of money, that the conceptual art was going to be the blueprint for creating a world that would astonish audiences and be fully believable to them."

"We had to do a presentation to New Line," recalls Dennis Gassner, "because everybody was concerned about what the movie was going to look like. I found myself jetting out of the gates in a crazy horse race, and I don't think I've ever ridden as fast — speeding around the course in the hope of reaching the finishing line!"

Movie Storyboards

The storyboard was first used in the Walt Disney animation studios in the early years of sound pictures. Before its introduction, the company's artists used story-sketches to outline the action in a film. Eventually someone got the idea of pinning the sketches onto boards, which meant that the visual script for the film was suddenly portable and could be transported to script meetings or to the rooms of the various animators. It also meant that the story could easily be changed — an individual drawing could be moved to somewhere else, thrown out, or substituted with another sketch altogether. The storyboard was rapidly adopted throughout the movie industry. It was famously used to plan scenes in *Gone With the Wind,* and is used today on all action and special effects movies — including *The Golden Compass.*

His Dark Materials - "The Golden Compass"

Description:
... Lyra watches in horror although Ragnar is now encumbered.

Chris Weitz Approved
Scene #: **153** *
Panel #: 26
Date: 29th June 2006
Jonathan Millward

Description:
The chainmail still attached but hanging loose ...

Chris Weitz Approved
Scene #: **153** *
Panel #: 27
Date: 29th June 2006
Jonathan Millward

Description:
Iorek is worse off.... He is bleeding from his neck and is panting heavily. CAM tracks with him.

Chris Weitz Approved
Scene #: **153** *
Panel #: 28A
Date: 29th June 2006
Jonathan Millward

Description:
Until his is adjacent with Lyra ...
Lyra- " Oh Iorek ! "
CAM comes round Iorek and floats up, as he unsteadily rises to his feet.

Chris Weitz Approved
Scene #: **153** *
Panel #: 28B
Date: 29th June 2006
Jonathan Millward

◄ *On The Golden Compass movie, each shot of the terrifying battle between the Ice Bear Iorek Byrnison and his archenemy Ragnar was planned out using storyboards.*

In addition to the many examples of concept art and 3-D concept models of characters and creatures, a full "storyboard" was made of the script. As the name suggests, a storyboard is a large board — or a series of boards — onto which hundreds of sketches can be pinned that tell the story of a film in pictorial form.

"We were very vigilant in our preproduction process," says Deborah Forte, "and every frame of the movie was storyboarded. This meant that we were able to calculate whether or not our plan was achievable and what had to be altered or adjusted before anything had been filmed."

Deborah delivered her response to New Line's challenge, and suddenly the film moved from being a possible project to a real but demanding undertaking.

"Deborah spent a decade trying to get this movie made," says Chris Weitz. "She has been the caretaker of Philip Pullman's legacy in terms of seeing it realized on the screen and has managed to keep going through all kinds of ups and downs. It's hard to get any movie off the ground, but something this size is extraordinarily difficult and when we got the green light, I think it was a huge moment for her and for all of us. It was a big deal!"

Making Maquettes

Following the creation of the initial concept art for the Ice Bears, highly detailed scale-models of the animals were made. Concept models such as these — also called maquettes — are a useful way of showing a design concept in three dimensions. In the case of the Ice Bears, the maquettes also highlight the physical and facial differences between Iorek Byrnison (above left) and his larger rival Ragnar Sturlusson (above right).

▶ ▼ *All of the amazing creatures seen in The Golden Compass were created using computer-generated imagery. The Ice Bears were developed by Framestore CFC, a UK-based company, working under the movie's Visual Effects Supervisor, Mike Fink. Iorek Byrnison (right and below top) was designed to appear considerably smaller than his arch rival, Ragnar Sturlusson (below bottom). The two bears also have distinctive, individual muzzle shapes.*

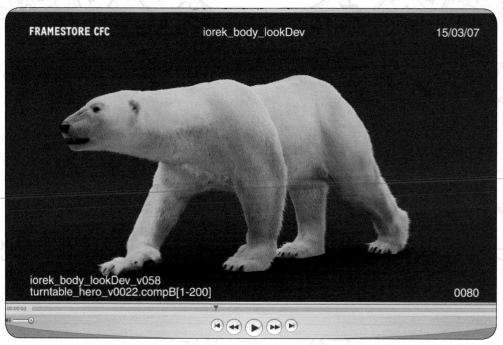

▶ *The insectlike spy-flies (right) are highly detailed examples of CGI. Each spy-fly features intricate wings, which open to reveal a green casing that houses an evil spirit – the sinister force powering the device.*

Animating the Ice Bears

When it came to animating the talking, armored Ice Bears, Mike Fink undertook specific research. "The idea was to keep Iorek (left) and the other bears as animal-like as possible. For example, when they talk, we didn't want them to move their mouths in the way that humans do," says Mike. "I met with experts at the Royal Veterinary College and talked with them about animal musculature. I wanted to know whether any animals have a physical structure that could enable them to speak and, if so, how that speech would manifest itself." This discussion resulted in some surprising facts, as Mike explains: "In most cases, animals simply don't modulate the wind going past their larynx in a way that makes sufficient tones to produce speech. However, some animals do, among them bears, which have the necessary physical ability to be vocal but are not because it isn't in their genes. But, structurally, they could do it!"

One of the greatest challenges facing Visual Effects Supervisor Mike Fink during the presentation to New Line Cinema was to convince the studio that it was possible to deliver the complex range of special effects on which *The Golden Compass* would be dependent. The Ice Bears and shape-changing dæmons seen in the movie were created using computer-generated imagery (CGI). This process took many months of intensive work by visual effects teams at three separate CGI companies in both the United States and the United Kingdom — Rhythm and Hues (California, U.S.), Cinesite (Shepperton Studios and London, UK) and Framestore CFC (London, UK). Fink recalls the pressure: "Other films with furry creatures had people working on the effects a year and a half before they even started to shoot the movie. We had a matter of months to get up to speed."

But however elaborate and convincing the special effects, none of them would be worth anything without the underlying narrative structure. "It might have been possible," says Chris Weitz, "to sell something on sheer spectacle, but audiences are now so familiar with what can be achieved with visual effects that it still comes back to the same old stuff — a good story and convincing characters." Mike Fink agrees: "What none of us could ever afford to forget was that this is a personal story: We had always to remember that, at its heart, *The Golden Compass* is Lyra Belacqua's story."

And eventually the time came when someone had to be found to play Lyra Belacqua....

▶ *A wide range of computer-generated animal forms were created for the dæmons seen in* The Golden Compass *movie (right). The dæmon forms include the Jordan College librarian's raccoon, John Faa's crow, Fra Pavel's chameleon, and Lord Asriel's snow leopard.*

LOOKING FOR LYRA

Casting the Movie — The Search for a Heroine

"Search For Actress To Play 'Lyra Belacqua' Comes To Four UK Cities — Cambridge, Kendal, Oxford and Exeter." In March 2006, this announcement heralded the beginning of a nationwide casting search to find a young actress to play the lead role of Lyra Belacqua in the movie adaptation of *The Golden Compass*. The official press release (pictured right) appeared in several British newspapers and created a great deal of excitement among would-be Lyras across the nation.

Deborah Forte had always hoped to find someone for the role of Lyra from an "open casting call" at which members of the public can try out for a role. "I wanted to find someone," she says, "who could come to this part fresh and enthusiastic and not be labeled as an actor from another film. However, the production schedule called for Lyra to be on set for all but a couple of days out of nearly 100 days of shooting. The decision to put an inexperienced actress in the part might have seemed questionable, but fortunately New Line supported us in that decision."

For Chris Weitz, "There were a number of things that had to be right about *The Golden Compass*, or the film would fail utterly. The look of the film had to be right, the dæmons had to be right, and, above all, Lyra had to be right. The look and the dæmons were elements that we could shape and refine, but when it came to casting someone to play Lyra, we knew that we were going to have to choose one particular human being, who might or might not be suitable for the part."

Casting directors Lucy Bevan and Fiona Weir arranged open auditions in Oxford, Cambridge, Exeter, and the Cumbrian town of Kendal. The result was that 10,000 girls turned up to audition for the role of Lyra.

NEW LINE CINEMA ANNOUNCES OPEN UK CASTING CALLS FOR LEAD ROLE IN

"THE GOLDEN COMPASS"

Search For Actress To Play "Lyra Belacqua" Comes To Four UK Cities – Cambridge, Kendal, Oxford and Exeter - starting April 4th.

LONDON, MONDAY MARCH 13TH, 2006: New Line Cinema, the studio behind the Oscar®-winning LORD OF THE RINGS trilogy, has launched a nationwide casting search in the UK to find a young actress to play the lead role of **Lyra Belacqua** in the highly anticipated feature film adaptation of Philip Pullman's bestselling novel *The Golden Compass*, it was announced today by New Line Cinema and producer Deborah Forte.

Lyra Belacqua, is one of the most beloved and spirited characters in children's literature, and like her creator, a born storyteller. *The Golden Compass* casting directors Fiona Weir and Lucy Bevan are looking for a talented young actress who embodies Lyra's loyalty, bravery and mischievous nature.

The initial open casting calls will take place in Cambridge, Kendal (in the Lake District), Oxford and Exeter during the first two weeks of April and are open to girls between the ages of nine and thirteen who are accompanied by a parent or guardian and resident in the UK. Applicants will be asked to complete a form and may be seen briefly by one of the casting directors. Children should come as themselves (no costumes or makeup allowed), dress warmly, and be prepared to wait. No previous acting experience is required. The Casting Calls, with queues open from 10am to 2pm and a 5pm close of the Call, will take place as follows:

DATE	CITY	VENUE
April 4	Cambridge	The Corn Exchange
April 6	Kendal	The Cattle Green Hotel
April 11	Oxford	The Examination School, The High Street
April 13	Exeter	The Great Hall, University Of Exeter

Based on the bestselling, award-winning and critically acclaimed Pullman novels, the *His Dark Materials* trilogy is comprised of *The Golden Compass*, *The Subtle Knife*, and *The Amber Spyglass*. It revolves around a young girl (Lyra) who travels to the far north to save her best friend. Along the way, she encounters shape-shifting creatures, witches, and a variety of otherworldly characters in parallel universes. THE GOLDEN COMPASS is produced by Deborah Forte of Scholastic Media.

▲ *"I really wanted to be Lyra,"* says Dakota Blue Richards. *"If somebody had said that I could play any part in the world, that would have been the part I would have chosen."*

The Author's Choice

During the casting of Lyra, Deborah Forte sent Philip Pullman a DVD showing the auditions of the 40 girls shortlisted for the role. Within 48 hours, the author telephoned Deborah and said, "It's one of two girls...." As Deborah says, "What was fascinating was that the two girls he picked were among those that I had already singled out." And one of them was Dakota Blue Richards. Looking back on the would-be Lyras, Pullman's view is that: "Many of them had one Lyra-like quality, some had a few, but only Dakota Blue Richards had them all."

One of them was a twelve-year-old Brighton schoolgirl, Dakota Blue Richards. A friend of Dakota's mother had seen an item on children's television about the auditions and, knowing that Dakota was a fan of the books, passed on the information. So Dakota decided to attend the very first of the audition calls to be held at The Corn Exchange in Cambridge on April 4, 2006. "It really wasn't a big decision," she says. "I just thought I'll have a go...."

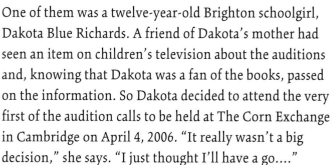

"Many of them had one Lyra-like quality, some had a few, but only Dakota Blue Richards had them all."

PHILIP PULLMAN

Dakota had some stage experience, having been in school plays and one or two local amateur-theater productions, but the chances of getting the part seemed slim. As Dakota remembers: "Standing in line with 3,000 other girls at eight o'clock on a freezing-cold morning, I couldn't imagine what it would be like if I got the part. I didn't think I had a chance." In batches of 50 or more at a time, the would-be Lyras filed into a big hall. "We had to give our name, age, and where we came from," says Dakota, "and then answer a couple of questions. They asked us, 'What would your dæmon be?' and I think I said a cat, but if I was asked now I would probably say a ring-tailed lemur."

Some of the girls, including Dakota, had their photographs taken and were asked to read a couple of scenes from the film, including Lyra's first meeting with the Ice Bear Iorek Byrnison. "I really wasn't nervous," she remembers, "because it was just about that one audition. I really didn't think I was going to get it — I didn't even expect to be recalled."

But Dakota was recalled as part of a group of 40 girls who met the casting directors in a Soho office in the heart of London's theaterland. This time, in addition to acting several more scenes from the screenplay in front of a camera, the Lyra-hopefuls had to do an improvisation.

Filming Dakota

"Dakota has a very open-looking face — it's to do with where her eyes are positioned in her head," says Director of Photography Henry Braham. "It's one of the reasons why she's so mesmerizing on the movie screen and why the character of Lyra Belacqua seems so very accessible."

"We had to act as if we were in a dark room," recalls Dakota, "and there were two doors, one on each side of the room. Then we had to imagine that behind one door we could hear children's voices and behind the other nothing but the sound of the wind." Once again, Dakota left the audition thinking that the next thing she'd hear about *The Golden Compass* would be when it opened at her local cinema!

However, various important people were intently viewing the latest round of auditions and one of them was Deborah Forte. Impressed by Dakota, the producer shortlisted her with seven other hopefuls. When, a few weeks later, the eight girls auditioned for Chris Weitz, Dakota made an equally strong impression on the director. Dakota and one other girl were called to Shepperton film studios to do a screen test with hair, make-up and costume. "That was probably the scariest part of all," says Dakota. "It was scary in itself, but then, suddenly, there was the added worry that after all this I might not get it anyway!" She needn't have worried. "The minute Dakota came to do the screen test," says Deborah Forte, "we knew: We didn't even have to see the screen test to know that she was the right girl."

So, what was it about Dakota that made such a strong impression? "First and foremost," says Chris Weitz, "Dakota was the person who felt right for the role — something I had felt when I had looked at the video-recording of her very first audition — but working with her I realized that she was able to take direction and that she's thoughtful, clever, and spirited in the same way as the character in Philip Pullman's books." For Deborah Forte, Dakota's "look" and her personality were also key factors: "She was beautiful in a very unconventional way and had this feral quality to her that the other girls didn't have. She was very natural, had total confidence, and was also bravely unsentimental. There is a lot of Lyra in Dakota!"

"They telephoned to say I had the part," remembers Dakota, "but I still didn't really believe it was happening. In fact, it wasn't until I did the very first shot of the whole movie that I suddenly went, 'Aaaaaghh! This is real! I'm doing it!'"

While the search for Lyra was being conducted, other important discussions were taking place to complete the rest of the cast list and, in particular, to fill the key roles of Mrs. Coulter and Lord Asriel….

BEARS, WITCHES, HEROES, AND VILLAINS

Casting the Movie – Characters and Creatures

From the outset, Deborah Forte and Philip Pullman were both agreed about who would be the ideal actress to play Mrs. Coulter. "Every producer," says Deborah, "indulges in what we call fantasy casting: 'Oh,' we say, 'if only we could get so-and-so for this part or that....'" Pullman recalls those games of fantasy casting: "I wanted Nicole Kidman for the part of Mrs. Coulter," he says, "and Laurence Olivier, circa 1945, for Lord Asriel." The dream of casting the late Sir Laurence Olivier, who had played rugged and romantic roles in the 1930s and '40s in such films as *Wuthering Heights* and *Pride and Prejudice*, was clearly not an option.

But Nicole Kidman — Philip and Deborah's first choice for Mrs. Coulter — was very much alive and, as a Hollywood superstar, incredibly in demand. It was an ambitious piece of fantasy casting, but the Oscar®, Golden Globe®, and BAFTA winner, whose credits ranged through a diversity of movies — including *Batman Forever*, *The Portrait of a Lady*, *Eyes Wide Shut*, *Moulin Rouge!*, *The Hours*, *Cold Mountain*, and *Bewitched* — had read Philip Pullman's *His Dark Materials* trilogy and accepted the role.

◄ ▶ *Nicole Kidman, Dakota Blue Richards, and Sam Elliot worked closely with Director Chris Weitz on their characters and performances during the filming of* The Golden Compass.

"The original material became the attraction," explains Deborah. "Nicole knew the books and wanted to be involved." For Chris Weitz, Nicole's agreement to accept the role of Mrs. Coulter felt like a fabulously lucky break. "Nicole brought complete commitment to what other actors might have viewed as a kind of 'fun turn' as a villain," he says. Certainly with a different performer in the part, Mrs. Coulter might easily have become a caricature. "It would have been so easy to play it plain evil," continues Chris, "but Nicole, knowing and understanding the books, was determined that Marisa Coulter should be a fully human character. As a result, she comes across as formidable, sexually powerful, and ruthless, yet clearly vulnerable and damaged. That is a tough thing to pull off."

Philip Pullman is also full of praise for Nicole Kidman, describing her as having "the extraordinary quality of being able to play cold and warm, terrifying and seductive, all at the same time."

"Nicole brought complete commitment to what other actors might have viewed as a kind of 'fun turn' as a villain."

CHRIS WEITZ

With the casting of Olivier an impossibility, a lead actor also needed to be found to play Lord Asriel. Daniel Craig had impressed audiences and critics in such films as *Road to Perdition, Copenhagen, Sylvia,* and *Munich,* and was duly offered the role of Lyra's stern uncle. He accepted the part shortly before being propelled to international superstardom, following his casting as the latest incarnation of Ian Fleming's secret agent James Bond in the movie *Casino Royale*.

Becoming the new 007 presented several interesting challenges for Daniel — the shooting schedules for *The Golden Compass* and *Casino Royale* overlapped and he had to switch back and forth between being an Arctic explorer and a British MI6 agent! "Bond is going to occupy a lot of Daniel's life for a long time to come," says Chris Weitz, "so we were really fortunate to get him. Daniel is a good-looking man: not 'pretty boy' looks, but the romantic looks of a 19th-century literary hero. He is also highly intelligent and humorous and conveys those qualities. The schedule only called for Daniel to be on set

◄ *Nicole Kidman brings to life the mysterious character of Mrs. Coulter in* The Golden Compass *movie. The Oscar®-winning actress was Philip Pullman's first choice for the role.*

for thirteen days, but Lord Asriel's role in the story is incredibly important and we knew that with Daniel in the part, the character would stand astride the movie."

Once again, Philip Pullman was delighted with the casting: "Asriel," he says, "requires someone who has the physical presence of a man of action, the quick intelligence of a scholar, and the charisma to dominate the screen while apparently doing nothing. When Daniel Craig was mentioned, I leapt at the idea and he is ideal."

The role of the Witch Queen, Serafina Pekkala, went to French actress Eva Green, who followed a successful stage career with a striking film-debut performance in *The Dreamers* for the Italian director Bernardo Bertolucci. She then went on to costar with Orlando Bloom and Liam Neeson in Ridley Scott's *Kingdom of Heaven*. Curiously, Eva's next role brought her into contact with Lord Asriel — or more accurately Daniel Craig — when she was cast opposite him as "Bond girl" Vesper Lynd in *Casino Royale*.

The casting process differs from artist to artist: Some actors are invited to audition, while major stars tend to be cast by "offer only," meaning that the producers and director are employing an actor on the strength of his or her track record and past successes.

▲ Eva Green plays Serafina Pekkala, the Clan-queen of the Witches of Lake Enara.

▶ Cast as Lord Asriel, Daniel Craig delivers a commanding performance as the rugged adventurer.

ROYAL INST. ARCTIC

SVALBARD

"You are trying to assemble a strong creative lineup," says Chris, "while attempting to balance the demands on the budget and the schedule. The result is ten to a dozen negotiation processes all going on simultaneously; but once you start getting really good people, you get greedy and want more and more excellent actors!"

"As hard as it was getting this movie up and running," notes Deborah Forte, "and even though it seemed that every conceivable obstacle that could present itself against us did so, the casting came together and worked out to perfection."

A good example of achieving that perfection is the casting of Emmy® and Golden Globe®-nominated actor Sam Elliott as the courageous aeronaut-for-hire Lee Scoresby. The character of Scoresby was based on the heroic Wild West "cowboy" figure seen in countless Hollywood movies. A three-time winner of the Western Heritage Award, Sam has created a number of memorable Western roles for television and cinema, including the legendary gunfighter Wild Bill Hickok, in the made-for-TV movie *Buffalo Girls*.

"Once you start getting really good people, you get greedy and want more and more excellent actors!"

CHRIS WEITZ

"Sam Elliott," says Chris Weitz, "was born to play Lee Scoresby." Deborah Forte agrees: "Sam is just fantastic! He is the quintessential cowboy. When he heard that we were filming in the United Kingdom, he was afraid that we wouldn't get it right, but once we'd satisfied him that his costume and guns were going to look authentic, he trusted us and brought to the movie his own unique understanding of the Western experience."

▶ *Sam Elliot, a veteran of numerous Western television series and movies, was the ideal choice for Philip Pullman's cowboy-style hero, Lee Scoresby.*

The Voice of Pantalaimon

Born in London on February 14, 1992, Freddie Highmore (pictured left) was double nominated for a Screen Actors Guild Award for his performance as Peter Llewelyn Davies — the boy who inspired the book *Peter Pan* — in the movie *Finding Neverland*. His co-star, Johnny Depp, recommended him for the role of Charlie Bucket in the film adaptation of Roald Dahl's classic children's book, *Charlie and the Chocolate Factory*, for which Freddie won the BFCA Best Young Actor's Award for the second time in a row. Freddie has also appeared opposite Russell Crowe in *A Good Year* and opposite real baby tigers in *Two Brothers*. Fred played the title roles in *August Rush*, alongside Robin Williams, and also in the movie *Arthur and the Invisibles*, which was part live action and part voiceover work. This proved to be invaluable experience when he finally won the coveted role of the voice of Lyra's dæmon, Pantalaimon, in *The Golden Compass*. In his next movie, Freddie will be appearing opposite himself as he plays twins in an adaptation of *The Spiderwick Chronicles*.

▶ *The talented cast of* The Golden Compass *features Simon McBurney as the Magisterial agent Fra Pavel (near right); Jack Shepherd as the Master of Jordan College (middle right); and Ben Walker as Roger Parslow (far right), Lyra's friend in Oxford.*

Some of Britain's top stage, film, and TV actors completed the cast, including Sir Tom Courtenay as Farder Coram, the wise Elder of the Gyptian clan who was once in love with the witch Serafina Pekkala; Jim Carter as John Faa, King of the Gyptians; Clare Higgins as Ma Costa; Jack Shepherd as the Master of Jordan College; and Simon McBurney as Fra Pavel.

Equal concern was paid to the casting of the voice talent in *The Golden Compass*. One of the outstanding artists who contributed to the movie was Golden Globe®-winner Ian McShane as the growling, roaring voice of Ragnar Sturlusson — the King of the Ice Bears. "I look at our cast now," says a satisfied Deborah Forte, "and I just say to myself, 'They're perfect!'"

The Gyptians

Descended from nomadic traders and warriors from the East, the Gyptian people are waterfarers who live on canal boats. They befriend Lyra and she travels with them to the North to rescue all of the children — both Gyptian and non-Gyptian — who have been abducted by the mysterious Gobblers.

◀ *Jim Carter as John Faa (far left); Sir Tom Courtenay as Farder Coram (middle left); and Clare Higgins as Ma Costa (near left).*

THE JOURNEY BEGINS

Filming on Location – From Oxford to the North Pole

"No one in my family had ever been to university before," wrote Philip Pullman, "never mind Oxford or Cambridge, but I wanted to go, and that was that." And go he did, reading English at Exeter College, Oxford, and later setting the beginning of *The Golden Compass* in a city of the same name. Lyra's Oxford in *His Dark Materials* is similar in some respects to the Oxford of our world, and so it was important to the filmmakers that the opening scenes of the movie should evoke the mood and atmosphere of the celebrated university city.

"If you were to take a tour of Oxford with Philip Pullman," says Producer, Deborah Forte, "he would take you, as he did us, to a variety of places in the city and you would begin to see the story come to life."

"A lot of the places," she continues, "such as the Master's Garden at Philip's old college, Exeter, are private and unknown to tourists. Partly because they are not accessible to the public, they have a mysterious, ancient quality to them that is almost fantastical. Visiting these places and experiencing how close they were to the spirit of the book made it essential for us to be able to shoot there."

Getting agreement to film in these exclusive locations — many of which had never before been invaded by film crews — required much delicate negotiation on behalf of the filmmakers. But perhaps because of Philip Pullman's reputation within the community — he is an Honorary Freeman of the City — permissions were granted and a week's filming in Oxford became an essential part of the movie's busy shooting schedule.

▶ *Exeter College in Oxford (right) was used for the filming of exterior scenes set at the fictional Jordan College in Lyra's world.*

◀ *The Historic Docks at Chatham in Surrey was the location for the busy Northern port of Trollesund.*

Shots were carefully planned so that, after filming, additional details could be created and added using computer graphics. "Our aim," says Visual Effects Supervisor Mike Fink, "was to make Oxford look just a little more magical. So we planned to change a few things around: adding more glass to some of the buildings and putting in a few buildings that aren't really there!" The Sky Ferry, for example, that takes Lyra and Mrs. Coulter to London appears to be moored in Tom Quad, the vast courtyard located in the center of Christ Church, Oxford (top left). The college was also home to another famous writer of fantasy — Lewis Carroll.

There are many historic dining halls in the various colleges of Oxford, but the location chosen for the scenes in the Dining Hall of Jordan College — where Lyra first meets Mrs. Coulter — was found not in Oxford but in the Painted Hall of the Old Royal Naval College (middle left), which stands beside the River Thames at Greenwich in London. The exterior of the building also provided the location for the headquarters of the Magisterium — the sinister organization that runs Lyra's world (bottom left).

Other London locations included some buildings and streets around Piccadilly Circus and the interior of the Park Lane Hotel, which was built in the 1920s and decorated in what was then the highly fashionable Art Deco style. For Production Designer Dennis Gassner, it was the only place to film the scene in which Mrs. Coulter takes Lyra to dinner at a sophisticated London restaurant.

◄ Concept art of the Magisterial Sky Ferry docked at Jordan College (top left); Lyra walks through the College Dining Hall (middle left); at the Magisterial Seat, Fra Pavel, and Mrs. Coulter formulate a plan to find Lyra and retrieve the alethiometer (bottom left).

"I was trained," explains Dennis, "by Dean Tavoularis, who was the Oscar®-winning designer on Francis Ford Coppola's *The Godfather* trilogy. He taught me to appreciate the Art Deco style. During my studies I had seen photographs of the Park Lane Hotel and had stored those images somewhere at the back of my brain. So when we came to think about the restaurant scene, I said, 'There's only one place where that's going to be shot and that's the Park Lane Hotel!'"

▼ *Dennis Gassner's elegant conceptualization of Lyra's London was inspired by Sir Christopher Wren's plans to rebuild the city.*

▲ *The London dining scenes in* The Golden Compass *were shot at the Park Lane Hotel.*

For the most part, the London of *The Golden Compass* was conceived as being a "virtual city," created on a computer, although Dennis's designs drew their inspiration from a historical fact about the real city. "After the Great Fire of London," he explains, "King Charles II asked Christopher Wren to redesign London, which he did, although he was never able to put all of his plans into practice. However, Wren did rebuild St. Paul's Cathedral.

So I said, 'Let's take St. Paul's as his signature and reinvent London along the lines envisaged by Wren, but making more use of glass and metal rather than brick and stone.' The London visited by Lyra is a homage to a piece of genuine London history, which is all part of the fun of discovering a film."

◄ *Chris Weitz and Dennis Gassner discuss a scene while on location shooting* The Golden Compass.

For exterior scenes set in the Northern port of Trollesund, Director Chris Weitz decided to shoot at the Historic Docks in Chatham, Kent, to give the action a maritime feel. For even more authenticity, Weitz originally wanted to film the movie's icy, northernmost scenes in the Arctic. Although some snow scenes were eventually shot in Switzerland, the desire to film at the North Pole proved impractical. "The budget was one factor," he explains, "but we also ran up against the reality of the law and the fact that we were only going to be able to work with Dakota for four hours of actual shooting each day."

> "Arctic light has an ethereal quality to it, especially at night in the summer when the sun never fully sets...."
>
> HENRY BRAHAM

The solution to this dilemma was to film the Arctic scenes in a studio using a visual effects technique called "greenscreen." The actors and the elements of the set are filmed against background screens of a single color — usually green. It then becomes possible, during post-production, to digitally replace the greenscreen background with other images to complete the scene.

For Director of Photography Henry Braham (below), the experience of shooting landscape photography in the Arctic — both for *The Golden Compass* and on the earlier TV series *Shackleton* — gave him an insight into the studio lighting effects that would be needed for the scenes set in the North. "Arctic light," he explains, "has an ethereal quality to it, especially at night in the summer when the sun never fully sets and there is a beautiful glow from the sky — which is not easy to re-create in the studio."

The ability to tackle such issues was the skill that Henry brought to the entire project, as he explains: "Chris Weitz and Dennis Gassner had really established the look of the physical world in the film, so what interested me was the question of how to tell Lyra's journey visually. And it seemed to me that you do that with the style in which you photograph it." Henry's approach was to explore *The Golden Compass* in terms of light and color. "We decided to simplify the coloring of the movie," he says, "so that there would be a real progression."

▼ At Shepperton Studios, the set of the Gyptian camp (below left) featured a painted backdrop to create the illusion of a mountainous background. Greenscreen backgrounds (below right) were also used in many shots.

"This movement," he continues, "begins in the warm, golden world of Oxford, which feels safe and comfortable, before we travel to the city of London and the glamorous, exciting world of Mrs. Coulter. In London, the coloring is a little more red and cream. Then, when Lyra finds herself being chased through the scarier parts of the city, the scenes are lit with a greenish tint, like old wartime photographs." This color journey continues as Lyra makes her escape. "Next," says Henry, "comes the period she spends with the Gyptians, which is bright and colorful in order to convey the sense of the excitement and expectation on beginning the voyage northwards. Trollesund, which is wintry and hard, is shot in browns and blues and uses a lot less color. Then, finally as we get into the world of ice and snow, the lighting uses various shades of blue to capture the cold but romantic world of the Arctic." This visual odyssey is also an emotional one, both for Lyra and the movie audience. "The shifting colors take you on the journey," says Henry. "You may not actually notice them, but they're just there underlining the emotion of the story."

W ith the locations for filming established, the effects under way, and the photographic approach agreed upon, work began on other key aspects of the movie's production. In addition to the creation of essential props — including the all-important alethiometer — the task of creating appropriate hair and makeup also got under way. But before the work of the props and makeup artists could be filmed, many hundreds of costumes needed to be designed and made, from elegant scholars' robes to the warm, fur-lined attire of polar explorers.

▶ *The various stages of Lyra's journey were filmed using different coloring and lighting. A green tint was applied when she is chased by the Gobblers in London (top right); warm colors were used during her time with the Gyptians (middle right); and in Trollesund, blue and brown color tones provide a wintry atmosphere (bottom right).*

FURS, TWEEDS, AND
A TOUCH OF GLAMOUR

Creating the Costumes for *The Golden Compass*

"It goes without saying," says Ruth Myers, the designer of the dazzling costumes created for *The Golden Compass*, "I LOVE my job!"

In fact, the sheer passion with which the Emmy® award-winning, multiple Oscar®-nominated designer talks about her stunning work on *The Golden Compass* leaves the listener in no doubt how she feels about her chosen career. When describing the business of designing and making the film's costumes, Ruth (pictured left) is hugely enthusiastic, and she talks about her "glorious," "amazing," and "absolutely delicious" fabrics as if they were alive — which, in a way, they become once the actors put them on and the cameras start rolling.

Ruth feels that her forty-year-long career in costume design — *LA Confidential, Emma, The Addams Family, Isadora,* and *Something Wicked This Way Comes* being just a few of her many films — has equipped her with the necessary expertise for the daunting task of creating the spectacular, varied range of costume styles that the project required. "Working on *The Golden Compass* has been fascinating to do," she says, "but I couldn't have done it ten years ago." "Everything I've done in my life," she continues, "has enabled me to arrive at the point where I can do this with some confidence." The diverse range of Ruth's career has meant that she has never been pigeonholed as a designer specializing in a particular period or style. This, as she explains, meant that she felt a natural attraction for the material: "I understood what Philip Pullman meant when he said that the world of *The Golden Compass* is this world, but it's also a different world. So, that was my approach: Some of my designs are almost-but-not-quite Edwardian or 1930s England; the Gyptians are almost-gypsies and the staff at the Magisterium wear uniforms that are not quite uniforms."

> *"I understood what Philip Pullman meant when he said that the world of **The Golden Compass** is this world, but it's also a different world."*
>
> RUTH MYERS

When Ruth had her first meeting with Director Chris Weitz and Production Designer Dennis Gassner, she found that they all shared a common vision on the visual approach for the creation of Lyra's world. "In fact," says Ruth, "within two or three weeks of our meeting it became obvious that we didn't have to talk to each other because we were on the same wavelength!"

◄ *Wearing a dazzling costume designed by Ruth Myers, Nicole Kidman makes a stunning entrance as Mrs. Coulter in* The Golden Compass.

Ruth began — where Philip Pullman's book begins — with Lyra Belacqua, the willful heroine of the film. "It's Lyra's story," she says, "Lyra's journey. The question was where to start with her; I knew if we could get that right we could go anywhere. Lyra's appearance is a good example of the film's 'period–no period' design. I didn't want her to look too *Alice in Wonderland*, I wanted to keep a sense that she could almost be a modern child."
Lyra starts out in what Ruth calls a run-down "smocky dress" that could have been worn in the past but which wouldn't look bizarre if a child wore it today. Then, as she explains, she added the twist: "Rather than period shoes, I gave Lyra a pair of modern work boots. This was hugely important as it's a way of entwining the worlds together."

▲ Lyra's modern boots and old-fashioned smock contrast with Lord Asriel's smart, Edwardian-style tweed suit.

Choosing a range of colors for a character — the "color palette" — is a vital part of the design process. Lyra's color palette starts off in Oxford with a series of cool shades of blue and red, which get colder during her time in London with Mrs. Coulter. Then, after Lyra leaves the city and joins the Gyptians, Ma Costa puts her in a

▲ The woollen coat given to Lyra by Ma Costa has a warm, textured feel that complements Lyra's character.

◄ ▲ *The colorful diversity of the Gyptian costumes reflects the different ethnic origins of members of the Gyptian tribes.*

multicolored, knitted coat. "In order to get an unusual texture and patterning," Ruth explains, "we experimented by knitting with all sorts of different materials and, in addition to wool, Lyra's coat contains ribbons and pieces of velvet and net, creating a look that is otherworldly."

At the same time, Ruth is adamant that "you can't just 'make it all up'! Even though it's a fantastic other world it has to be true to that world." Lyra's highly individual Gyptian coat will also help establish the character's image on film. "When you see her in the coat," notes Ruth, "it looks completely organic and part of her character."

▶ Ma Costa's warm and practical clothes are well suited for the hardy, traveling life of the Gyptians.

Lyra's coat is true to the design approach that Ruth followed for the look of all of the Gyptian people's clothes. The intention was that their garments should have a very natural feel, and as a result they were made out of a variety of homespun materials, leather, and wool. Distinct costume styles were developed for the different Gyptian races seen in the film, incorporating Nordic, North African, Anglo-Saxon, and Spanish influences.

In developing these different styles, Ruth wanted to make a statement about the origins of the Gyptian characters seen in the film. The intention was to show that "they are all colorful and are not just a higgledy-piggledy group of gypsies — the clothing styles give a very clear sense of where the Gyptians came from."

According to Ruth, there are a couple of unwritten rules about costume design: "Firstly, you have to give each character an image that goes straight into everybody's minds; and, secondly, however wonderful the costumes are that you do for a film, essentially audiences only ever remember the first one they see on a character! This means that you really do have to go for broke at the very beginning because you can't go back to it — it's too late!" This is particularly true of the glamorous, character-defining outfit worn by Mrs. Coulter in her introductory scene when she attends a dinner at Jordan College (see page 46). "It simply shimmers!" says Ruth.

In *The Golden Compass* movie, Mrs. Coulter wears several different coats and jackets featuring fur-lined collars. "Wherever possible," says Ruth, "I've used fake furs, partly because I'm a vegetarian, but also because with so many scenes featuring dæmons it is a very 'animally' film. You can find wonderful man-made furs and, because they are not from real animals, they are far more magical."

▶ *Artificial furs were used to create the collar linings of Mrs. Coulter's coats and jackets.*

Design Sketches and Fabrics

All of Ruth's costume designs begin with sketches. "I start with a profile, a silhouette, and then I draw...." she says. Once she is satisfied with her rough pencil designs, she begins the process of selecting different fabrics. The designs below (from left to right) show Ruth's initial sketches and a sample of the material used; Lyra's woollen coat, Mrs. Coulter's "dinner at Jordan" outfit; the robes worn by the Master of Jordan College; a Tartar guard's uniform.

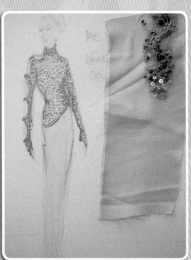

▲ *Mrs. Coulter's glamorous costumes were inspired by the styles and fashions of the 1930s and '40s.*

In contrast to the colorfulness of the Gyptians, the color palette used for Mrs. Coulter's clothes is very monochrome. With the exception of one scene at the Magisterium where she is dressed in a dark purple costume, she is typically seen in simple light or dark tones, such as cream, gold, gray, black, and white.

"With Mrs. Coulter," says Ruth, "I wanted her to look like the most unbelievably glamorous creature in the world. So, for my initial inspiration, I looked at fashions from the 1930s and '40s — which is when women were the most glamorous they have ever been — and played with those ideas in order to create a line, a sense of figure." She worked closely with Nicole Kidman to ensure that she had the actress's confidence and approval: "She is wonderful to dress. I sent her my drawings and she called me to say that she loved them and to go with whatever I wanted — which is a unique experience with an actress!"

Ruth loves working with actors, and it was through talking with Daniel Craig that she eventually settled on the look for Lord Asriel. " We both knew who he was and where we were going with him: Asriel was a real explorer: from a different era, but very English."

Tweed and Oilskins

Lord Asriel was the one character that presented Ruth Myers with difficulties. "I kept collecting bits and pieces of fabric," she remembers, "but I just couldn't 'get' what to do with Lord Asriel. Daniel Craig came in for a chat and he said, 'What about a tweed suit?' I had some wonderful tweed cloth that I'd been keeping, so I held up the fabric against him and everything made sense." As well as the tweed suit (left), Ruth also created a tough, warm, fur-and-oilskin outfit (right) for Asriel based on the clothing of early-20th-century polar explorers.

Painting Fabrics

The gown worn by the Master of Jordan College (right), like a great many costumes in the film, has a pattern painted directly onto the material. "Painting on costumes is much better than using ornate fabrics or having them embroidered," says Ruth. "I can create the look of the fabric for the camera by deciding how much patterning to show, whether I want it to look new or old and where I want light and shade."

On various projects in the past, Ruth has worked with a highly talented costume-making team, which she managed to reassemble for *The Golden Compass*. "We've spent a great deal of time painting and dyeing. It's very hard work but it's a fascinating process and we've all loved it because, in the end, we've created what are essentially our own fabrics." One of the most stunning examples of this process is the costume designed for the Queen of the Witches of Lake Enara, Serafina Pekkala. "We spent hours experimenting to find the right color," recalls Ruth. "We dyed it and re-dyed it until we arrived at something that is not a real color but a delicious dream color that is somewhere between indigo and purple and that I like to call 'The Color of the Night.' And when Eva Green flies through the air, her costume floats gloriously around her like a nighttime cloud."

As with all Ruth's designs, inspiration comes from many different sources. Serafina Pekkala's look owes something to the beautiful paintings of the 16th-century Italian artist Sandro Botticelli, with a nod to the work of the English Victorian painter Dante Gabriel Rossetti, together with "a hint of something Greek."

◄ As the Witch queen Serafina Pekkala, actress Eva Green wears a costume inspired by the work of the artists Botticelli and Rossetti.

▲ Many different uniforms are featured in The Golden Compass, including those worn by (from left to right) the officers of the Magisterial Police; the Trollesund Magisterial militia; the Tartar soldiers; the Magisterial Commissar, Fra Pavel.

"My main thought," she says, "was to ignore the word 'witch'; it never entered my head that she and the other witches would have pointed hats! I wanted to convey that their power was in their bodies, so I concentrated on a look that combined classical beauty with an unearthly supernatural quality and a sense of the magical."

Working on The Golden Compass has included some tough challenges — notably, Ruth confesses with a laugh, the uniforms. "I've always been terribly bad at uniforms!" Several different types of uniform were required, including the cold, threatening mid-gray uniforms of the Magisterial Police, designed to be reminiscent of those worn in Nazi Germany. For the fearsome Tartar soldiers, Ruth mixed elements of "Cossack costumes and American footballers' gear" to give a feeling of superhuman strength and power. A heavy, dark gray color was used, inspired by the fact that the soldiers are accompanied by wolf-dæmons. "It's given me an incredible kick to think that I've created my very own personal army!" laughs Ruth.

Ruth Myers has worked on many big films, but nothing, she readily admits, has ever involved the sheer variety and scale as her work for The Golden Compass. These range from creating an iconic cowboy image for Lee Scoresby (incorporating the suggestions of actor Sam Elliott, who insisted on wearing a bandana because he felt that without one Scoresby wouldn't be a proper cowboy!) through to designing in "assorted ice-cream colors" the pajamas worn by the children escaping from the sinister Bolvangar station.

"Philip Pullman paid me the best compliment I've ever had in my life," says Ruth, summing up the experience. "He looked at the costumes and said, 'This is my world, but more so than I could ever have imagined.' That was a wonderful, wonderful thing to say...."

◄ The costume worn by the heroic aeronaut Lee Scoresby – played by Sam Elliot – was based on the look of a 19th-century American cowboy.

TARTAR BEARDS AND GYPTIAN TATTOOS

Hair and Makeup Design for Lyra's World

"No more beards! That's what I said!" Peter King — the hair and make-up artist on *The Golden Compass* — is recalling his experiences working on *The Lord of The Rings* trilogy, for which he won a well-deserved Oscar®. After three years of putting facial hair on Gandalf, Gimli, and Saruman, Peter was well and truly through with beards. Or so he thought — when we met during his lunch break in a makeup room at Shepperton Studios, Peter (pictured below) had just spent the morning putting beards on an army of Tartar warriors!

"They're an army," he says, "so they all wear exactly the same costume — a uniform. There's a uniformity to their look, too, which is that of men who have spent most of their time out in the snow and have skin that is wind-burnt and chapped by the cold. But I've managed to give the Tartar soldiers some sense of individuality with their beards. There are blond beards, dark beards, and ginger beards, cut and trimmed in a variety of shapes — curly, square, pointed, or divided in the middle."

◀ *Many of the Gyptian characters were given intricate facial tattoos, braiding, and woven-in hair extensions.*

Although these soldiers are called Tartars, they do not resemble the 13th-century horsemen who followed Ghenghis Khan. They are closer to Cossacks, the race who became the most feared soldiers of the Russian Empire. Initially, the intention was to find bearded actors to play the Tartars, but then Director Chris Weitz requested that the soldiers should be played by ex-servicemen. The idea was that such actors would know what it is like to be part of an army, as well as having the right physical build and the ability to be convincing as aggressive warriors.

▼ *For the fierce Tartars, Peter King applied a variety of beards in different shapes and colors.*

"Chris was, of course, right," says Peter, "but, because ex-servicemen tend to be clean-shaven, I told him that his request was going to cost the film several thousand extra dollars in artificial beards! So, despite having said, 'No more beards!' here I am, back sticking hair on men's faces every day!"

Peter King first read *The Golden Compass* novel shortly after its publication and vividly recalls his first reaction. After reading only a few chapters of the book, he was convinced that it would make an amazing film. When Peter first met with Chris Weitz, they agreed that the overriding aim was to make the fantasy real and believable. "It helps," he says, "that it starts in Oxford in a world that seems almost familiar to us. The brilliance of Philip Pullman's writing and Dennis Gassner's designs for the production is that we think we recognize the world we are in and then realize that we don't!"

> "So, despite having said, 'No more beards!' here I am, back sticking hair on men's faces every day!"
>
> PETER KING

Although the opening scenes in Jordan College were relatively straightforward — most of the elder scholars having facial hair while the students were clean-shaven — Peter decided to add a detail that was unique to Jordan College men. "I wanted something," he says, "that would visually indicate that someone came from Jordan College. We toyed with outrageous ideas, such as having the back of the head shaved into a shape of some kind, but we finally settled on having everyone part their hair on the left-hand side. Of course, no one will ever notice!"

For Peter, the real pleasure of working on a story like *The Golden Compass* is that the flexibility of the setting allows the hair and makeup artists to concentrate on helping each actor to create their character, rather than

▲ *To create a unified look for the men of Jordan College, Peter King came up with the subtle idea of parting their hair on the left. The clean-shaven look of the students (above) was contrasted with the facial hair of the elder scholars.*

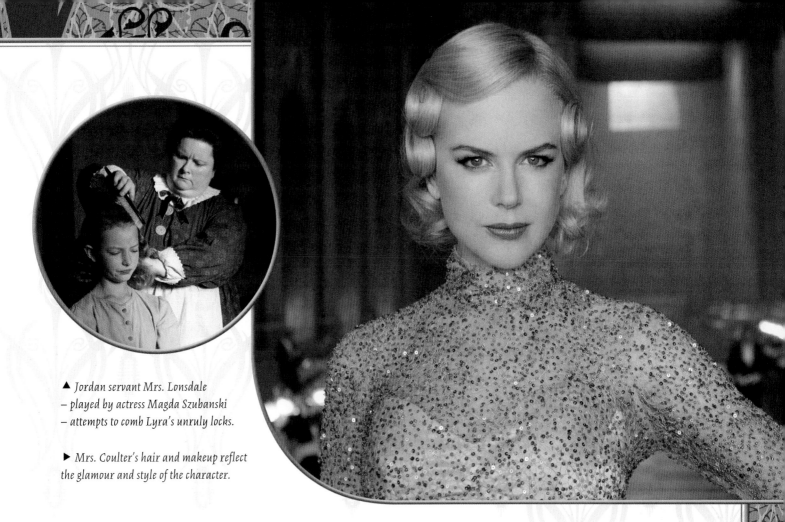

▲ Jordan servant Mrs. Lonsdale
– played by actress Magda Szubanski
– attempts to comb Lyra's unruly locks.

▶ Mrs. Coulter's hair and makeup reflect
the glamour and style of the character.

imposing a look that is locked into a specific historic period. "For example, I decided that Magda Szubanski's character, Mrs. Lonsdale — the Jordan servant who looks after Lyra — needed to have an Edwardian look because it seemed to fit with her *Upstairs, Downstairs* character and her fussy, nagging, heart-of-gold personality."

Once Lyra arrives in London and becomes part of Mrs. Coulter's sophisticated social set, the look was inspired by the 1930s. "Everything," says Peter King, "is incredibly sharp, chic, and stylish. Facial hair for the men does not exist! They have gelled-back, short-back-and-sides haircuts, but then we perked up their appearance with little unexpected touches such as a hint of mascara or a small diamond stud earring."

The real fun, however, came with devising the London women's hairstyles: "There was a team of ten really good hairdressers. I said to them that I wanted them to create their wildest fantasies, and that's exactly what we did, with hair piled up in towers or in great rolls or swirling cornucopia shapes."

> "Philip Pullman describes Mrs. Coulter as having long dark hair, but I wanted to make her ice-blond."
>
> PETER KING

When it came to Mrs. Coulter, who is the center of this high-society world, Peter took an approach that was contrary to the way in which the author depicted the character in his books. "Philip Pullman describes Mrs. Coulter as having long dark hair, but I wanted to make her ice-blond. I didn't want her appearance to be a cinematic cliché — villains always have dark hair — so I talked it over with Nicole Kidman and discussed how, if we gave her pale blond hair and the softest of makeups, we could make her look totally serene and unthreatening, as if butter wouldn't melt in her mouth; but then, when we begin to discover the kind of person she really is, she would seem far more chilling and sinister."

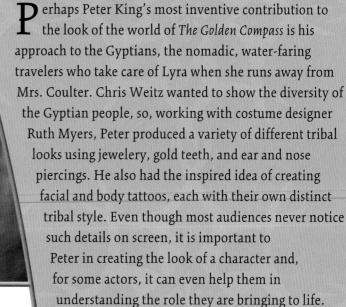

Perhaps Peter King's most inventive contribution to the look of the world of *The Golden Compass* is his approach to the Gyptians, the nomadic, water-faring travelers who take care of Lyra when she runs away from Mrs. Coulter. Chris Weitz wanted to show the diversity of the Gyptian people, so, working with costume designer Ruth Myers, Peter produced a variety of different tribal looks using jewelery, gold teeth, and ear and nose piercings. He also had the inspired idea of creating facial and body tattoos, each with their own distinct tribal style. Even though most audiences never notice such details on screen, it is important to Peter in creating the look of a character and, for some actors, it can even help them in understanding the role they are bringing to life.

"The women's tattoos," Peter continues, "are in a maroon, henna color. The men's are blue or black and those worn by the older Gyptians, like Farder Coram and John Faa, have been made to appear as if they have faded with age, while the younger characters' tattoos have a blacker, freshly inked look."

"When Philip Pullman first saw our initial ideas for the Gyptian makeup, he told me: 'Tattoos would never have entered my head, but seeing them, they look completely right!' That was very satisfying."

To re-create such complex makeup on a daily basis would have been very difficult — and a potential headache for film continuity — were it not for the fact that they were applied using special rub-down transfers. "We have sheets and sheets and sheets of them!" says Peter. "The company that produce them are superb, matching the patterns and colors of our designs and providing whatever specific detailing we request — sharp-edged outlines for the young people; softer, faded lines for the older characters — and with the great advantage that the whole thing can be put on an actor's face in two minutes dead!"

◀ *The younger Gyptians (top and middle left) have dark, fresh tattoos, while older characters such as John Faa (bottom left) have faded markings.*

Designing the Tattoos

The first challenge faced by Peter King in creating the Gyptian tattoos was deciding what they should look like. It was important, for example, that the tattoos shouldn't appear to be too closely inspired by the decoration of any ethnic groups in our world and — with the current popularity of body art — that they shouldn't look too modern.

Those concerns, combined with the fact that Production Designer Dennis Gassner was drawing part of his inspiration from the Art Deco design movement of the 1920s and 30s, led to Peter undertaking a great deal of research. The result was a wide range of tattoo ideas, from simple patterns of lines and dots for the Western Gyptians to ornate arrangements of curlicues for Eastern and Arabic Gyptians.

"Because the Gyptians travel on rivers and canals, several of the simpler designs consist of wavy lines representing water. I also looked up translations of the word 'water' in several different languages and designed various tattoos loosely inspired by the letters or characters of those words. One design features a triangle containing a disguised 'H' and two 'O's to represent H_2O, the molecular formula for water."

One of the actors who undergoes this treatment is Jim Carter, who plays Gyptian leader John Faa. As well as applying a slightly faded facial tattoo to indicate the character's age and status, Peter also applied other makeup techniques: "We turned Jim into an imposing figure: a huge bear of a man, with a big beard, gold teeth, and a grimy, dirty look as if he had coal dust in his eyes."

In contrast to the complexity of the Gyptian makeup, Peter opted for simplicity when it came to the race of witches who feature in *The Golden Compass*. The queen of the witches, Serafina Pekkala, is played by the actress Eva Green. "Everyone was wondering about the witch makeup," says Peter. "When we came to Eva Green's first appearance as Serafina Pekkala (pictured below), I could tell that everybody was waiting for some sort of 'witchy' look, but all I did was to turn her into the most beautiful, natural-looking woman ever. Eva was expecting to look more like a Goth warrior, with dark eyes and lips, but we went for something very different.

I wanted her to have a look that was timeless rather than of any specific age — and I was also absolutely adamant that she wouldn't look as if she'd been through the witches' beauty parlor!"

Witches, Gyptians, Tartars — it's all in a day's work for Peter King. "At least I don't have to worry about the bears," he laughs. "Can you imagine what it would be like if I was having to brush, dress, and curl the fur on several dozen giant polar bears each night! Beards are bad enough, but bears would be too much!"

GUNS, SPY-FLIES, AND GOLDEN COMPASSES

Making the Props and Decorating the Sets

I f you want to see the alethiometer, you need to talk to Prop Master Barry Gibbs (pictured below). During the shooting of *The Golden Compass*, the iconic device — or devices, as there are actually seven of them — were kept in a large, yellow-and-black industrial chest bolted to the floor of Barry's workshop at Shepperton Studios. Barry promises to unlock the chest — after he's revealed some of the other amazing gems stored away in the Aladdin's cave of wonders that is *The Golden Compass* Prop Master's stores at Shepperton.

"Props" — short for "properties"— are any objects carried or used by actors in a play or film, from a parasol to a pistol. The term also applies to all the furnishings that decorate the production's sets, such as lamps, paintings, and potted plants. "The normal role of a prop master," explains Barry, "is to work with the set decorator (see page 66) to track down and buy all the items needed on a film. But on *The Golden Compass* very little of what is seen on screen is quite like anything in our world. So on this film we've made everything we can and stamped our mark on everything else!"

◄ *A full-size polystyrene model of Iorek was used during the shooting of the scenes set in Trollesund.*

Stacked up in one corner of the workshop are 140 specially built wooden crates featuring intricate ethnic decoration, created for a scene in the Northern port of Trollesund. There's also a plastic, half-eaten joint of meat abandoned by the Ice Bear Iorek Byrnison, a tangled mass of rope and a wooden buoy from other scenes in the Norroway town. Several walls are covered with maps and charts of Lyra's world designed by graphics artist Jim Staines. These were created for scenes set in Lord Asriel's chambers and aboard the Gyptians' *Noorderlicht* ship, the Magisterial Sky Ferry and Lee Scoresby's airship. A luxurious carpet from Mrs.. Coulter's London home — hand-woven to an original design — is propped against a wall, and, standing on an easel, there is a striking portrait of the lady herself with her dæmon, the Golden Monkey.

▼ *Maps and charts of the world of* The Golden Compass *were specially created for the movie.*

On a nearby table sits Lord Asriel's leather-bound journal, a handful of Magisterium gold coins, and copies of the newspapers *The Daily Alethium* ("The Newspaper You Can Trust") and *The Magisterial News.* These mocked-up broadsheets carry such headlines as "Spy-Fly Plot Swatted: Blackmail Gang Crushed Like Bugs" and "Gyptians Kill And Eat Swan In London Park." Barry points out that "you won't be able to read those details on screen, but we enjoy putting in a lot of detail that only the actors will ever know are there!"

Other highly detailed items include a monogrammed pouch — seen in Lyra's bedroom in Mrs. Coulter's house — and cosmetic products used at the beauty parlor where Mrs. Coulter takes Lyra on her arrival in London. Each product was wrapped in pink and black packaging with Art Deco graphics and the brand name "Virginie, Paris–London." According to Barry, "It took 14 man-days to label all these products, and yet it is unlikely that anyone will ever notice them."

▲ *Newspapers and coins were made to add extra detail to Lyra's world.*
◄ *A pouch specially monogrammed with the letter "L" is one of several luxurious items seen in Lyra's bedroom in Mrs. Coulter's London home.*

In contrast to these barely glimpsed items, the spirit projector is a prop that will most certainly be seen on screen. This device — used by Lord Asriel to project a three-dimensional image of his discoveries at the North Pole — is an elegant piece of machinery in gleaming brass. "Originally," says Barry, "this was built simply as a film prop. Although it looks as if it is meant to function, it didn't contain any power or lightbulbs as we had expected that the projections shown by Lord Asriel would be created later with computer-generated imagery. Then, when Henry Braham joined the project as Director of Photography, he decided that he wanted the machine to project and so now it does — more or less successfully!"

◄ *In The Golden Compass, Lord Asriel's spirit projector machine projects 3-D images, or "photograms." These images are stored on spherical glass orbs kept in a special leather case.*

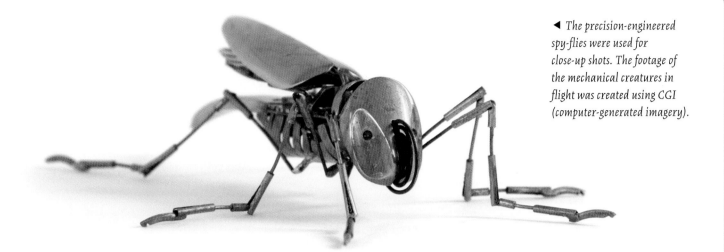

Fully equipped with an extensive range of tools and equipment, including a forge and lathes, Barry Gibbs's team of gifted craftspeople — graphic artists, sculptors, upholsterers, wood-, metal-, and leatherworkers — make or adapt the props required for the film. Props created by the team include the deadly spy-flies used by Mrs. Coulter to track down Lyra, as well as the beautifully tooled wooden box that contains the mechanical creatures. "We created a pair of spy-flies," says Barry, "that were precision-engineered with silver-plated carapaces and candy-lacquering to give their bodies a green, shimmering effect. One of the spy-flies was radio-controlled, so that when Mrs. Coulter removes the pin that holds the creature in the box, the spy-fly pops up and flutters its wings — after which the computer-generated effects take over."

Later on, this delicate and expensive prop had to undergo repairs as a result of a mishap on set. "The spy-fly was accidentally left switched on," explains Barry, "and every time anyone passed by with a remote control, the mechanism was triggered and the spy-fly tried to take off. Unfortunately, because the box lid was shut, the spy-fly virtually destroyed itself in its struggle to get free!"

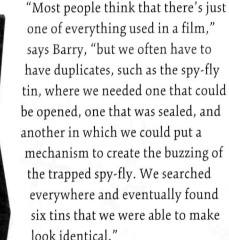

In one scene in *The Golden Compass*, the Gyptian elder Farder Coram traps one of the spy-flies in a tin. While browsing the Internet, Director Chris Weitz came across the perfect item to use as a prop — a Russian caviar tin. The tin, which had an unusual printed design featuring an image of a sturgeon, presented another challenge to Barry and his team.

"Most people think that there's just one of everything used in a film," says Barry, "but we often have to have duplicates, such as the spy-fly tin, where we needed one that could be opened, one that was sealed, and another in which we could put a mechanism to create the buzzing of the trapped spy-fly. We searched everywhere and eventually found six tins that we were able to make look identical."

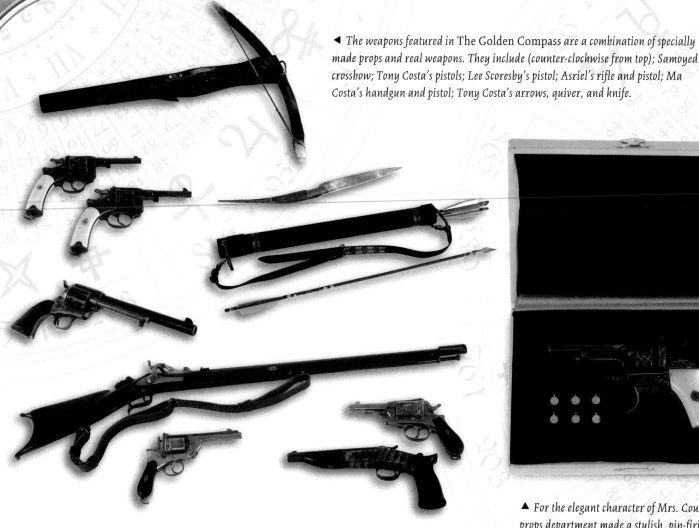

◄ The weapons featured in The Golden Compass *are a combination of specially made props and real weapons. They include (counter-clockwise from top); Samoyed crossbow; Tony Costa's pistols; Lee Scoresby's pistol; Asriel's rifle and pistol; Ma Costa's handgun and pistol; Tony Costa's arrows, quiver, and knife.*

▲ For the elegant character of Mrs. Coulter, the props department made a stylish, pin-firing pistol to reflect her glamorous but deadly nature. The beautifully designed weapon was contained in a monogrammed leather case, complete with an oil bottle and six rounds of ammunition.

Serafina's Cloud Pine Bow

The weaponry that involved the greatest amount of thought— and the most work in terms of design and manufacture — were the bows and arrows used by Serafina Pekkala and the witches. "We originally considered making the bows from glass," reveals Barry Gibbs, "but when the reference to the cloud pine used by the witches in order to fly was lost from the script, Chris Weitz decided that he wanted us to find a way to incorporate a reference to cloud pine in the design of Serafina's bow."

Experimentation began with attempts at grafting Christmas tree branches together, but then the decision was taken that the bow needed to be "practical" — a term used for a prop that isn't just seen on screen but also has to work. As a result, a bow was carved and a mold made so that extra bows could be cast in various materials. Lightweight, flexible versions were created for flying scenes and fully functioning bows were made for battle scenes. "To keep the cloud pine connection," says Barry, "we decorated the bows with sprigs of real pine that last for about two weeks and then have to be replaced."

◄ Serafina's bow was made from a molded, artificial material. Sprigs of pine were attached to the prop with glue.

All kinds of weapons were required for *The Golden Compass* movie, from Tartar swords to guns, rifles, knives, and crossbows. Some of these items were props, but many of them were real weapons from different time periods, supplied by Bapty & Co. Ltd., a specialist armorer used by the film and TV industries. Another important element unique to the world of *The Golden Compass* is "sky-iron," the hard-wearing metal from which the Ice Bears make their armor. The props department built a full-scale, polystyrene model of Iorek Byrnison and his armor in order to experiment with the texture and color of sky-iron. They used oxidized steel and bronze-colored paints to create a iridescent, reflective finish. A fifth-scale model was also made of the bear and his armor so that it could then be scanned into a computer for the reference of the digital effects artists.

Another full-size bear — standing upright on its hind legs — was sculpted in polystyrene to create a pattern for a series of inflatable, plastic bears. These were used on set to establish the type of lighting required for different scenes, and were designed to be inflated and deflated quickly.

◄ *The full-size model of Iorek's textured, interlocking armor was created from fiberglass.*

▼ *To create an iridescent, metallic effect, Iorek's armor was sprayed with various special types of paint.*

▼ *Full-size, inflatable bears were used to help the lighting crews set up shots on location and in the studio.*

▲ Finding objects such as these elegant perfume bottles (above left) is part of the Set Decorator's job. The Art Nouveau-style sculpture and rose-motif wallpaper (above right) were specially made for the movie.

Set Decoration

On a film as complex as The Golden Compass, the process of "dressing" the sets involves finding or making a great many things: furniture, curtains, lamps, the objects found on shelves, desks, and tables — even the wallpaper! "I begin by making a lot of lists," says Set Decorator Anna Pinnock (pictured left). "I spend a lot of time doing research in libraries and museums but, sooner or later, I have to start looking for all the things on those lists!"

Anna's lists include everything that needs to be used or seen within each of the sets, and if they can't be found, bought, or adapted, then they have to be made. For example, when the set was being designed for Lyra's attic bedroom in Oxford, Anna and her colleagues visited the Museum of Domestic Design & Architecture in Middlesex and studied their collection of wallpaper designs. "We found a paper we liked with a rose motif, but decided that we wanted it to have a more 'cartoony' feel, so we paid for the use of the design and then manipulated it into the exact look we wanted."

Every piece of baggage seen in the film was hand-made, including chests, trunks, cases, backpacks and, as Barry explains, a special desk designed to fold away for traveling that was created exclusively for Mrs. Coulter: "The designs called for a simple, stylish look with clean lines. I'm very proud of Mrs. Coulter's writing bureau."

Inspired by a design created by Louis Vuitton in the 1930s for the Russian-American conductor Leopold Stokowski, the bureau was made of cream leather. Opening it up, Barry reveals drawers and compartments containing an amazingly detailed collection of smaller props: monogrammed writing paper and envelopes, calling cards, a checkbook, a letter from Mrs. Coulter's bank (right) and various documents typed on an old-fashioned typewriter.

"This level of detailing," says Barry, "is intended to help the actor who uses them to feel more in character. What is particularly nice is being able to make things that are out of the ordinary."

▶ The fold-away writing bureau used by Mrs. Coulter was based on a Louis Vuitton design from the 1930s.

Creating the Alethiometer

"Originally, the alethiometer was going to be open-faced," says Barry. "The hands and interior workings were going to be created using CGI. Then the decision was taken that it would have a case — like an old pocket watch — and that it would actually have to work. We looked at a great many old watches, but it soon became clear that we were going to have to create the alethiometer entirely from scratch, partly so that it was completely unique to the film but also because it had to do what we needed it to do. It had to be the right size for Lyra to hold and handle comfortably and yet within its three-and-a-half-inch diameter size, it had to contain all the necessary mechanisms." In the end, seven alethiometers were made; two sealed "closed-case" props; three computerized versions; one operated by Lyra on screen; and a single camera-perfect copy used for what filmmakers call "beauty shots."

Director Chris Weitz suggested that the alethiometer's symbols should be colorful and have the look of decorations from a medieval manuscript. This challenge was solved by using the talents of Keith Seddon, a miniaturist who works for Fabergé. "To create a finished dial," says Barry, "was three days' work. The silver dial was machined to the artist's dimensions, filled with enamel — a process called hot enameling — and all the symbols were painted on by hand using brushes that are scarcely more than a few hairs thick." The casing was engraved with alchemical signs and calendar symbols as well as the spires of Prague, the European city where, it is said, the alethiometer was first created. Having made a working, perfect item, the alethiometer was "aged" because, as Barry explains: "Philip Pullman and Chris Weitz agreed that rather than looking new, the Compass had to look as if it had been handled and used over several hundred years."

I t would be difficult to think of a more out-of-the-ordinary object than the alethiometer and so Barry Gibbs finally unlocks the chest and displays what is the most significant — and valuable — prop in the film.

"When you're making a film prop," confides Barry, "you're normally trying to think of the quickest and easiest way of producing it rather than making a masterpiece. But this prop is also the name of the film, it is the Golden Compass, so we had to get it right." Having successfully made one alethiometer, it was necessary to repeat the process and create a device that could be seen to be working. The working Compass has three hands that Lyra can position on the appropriate symbols to ask a question, and a fourth answering hand operated by computer

▶ *Lord Asriel's intercision machine is another example of the skill and flair of Barry Gibbs' prop-making team.*

via a lead that enters the Compass, unseen, through its back. "It was then that we had an interesting experience," laughs Barry, "when someone said that it would be nice if the cogs and gears which could be seen inside the middle of the dial moved! So, it was back to the drawing board!"

A completely new case was made for the Compass and all the parts were remachined so that the device could be fitted with a set of moving gears and a motor to drive them.

Despite having been faced with so many problems, Barry clearly relishes his job: "I really love solving the challenge. You listen to someone saying we need this or that and then you have to rise to the challenge and go out and either find it or make it."

The stunning look of *The Golden Compass* owes much to the fact that Barry Gibbs and his team of designers and craftspeople have, again and again, met that challenge.

Lights! Camera! Action!

Filming in the Studio – Greenscreen and Visual Effects

Brrrrring! On the set of *The Golden Compass* at Shepperton Studios, an alarm bell rings loudly over the buzz of conversation and the chattering of the film crew begins to subside. "Nice and quiet, please!" shouts the First Assistant Director. "Settle down, now, everyone…. Shhh! No distractions!"

We are on "A" Stage, where the filming of a key scene is in progress. The film stage is packed with equipment, including cameras, sound-recording gear, TV monitors, laptop computers, snow and smoke machines, scaffolding, and ladders. Lengthy tangles of cables snake off in all directions, while banks of glaring white lights illuminate the set. There are a lot of people on the stage, from the First Assistant Director — who works with Director Chris Weitz to manage the smooth running of the filming — and his crew of technicians to the people responsible for costume, makeup, props, and set decoration. Runners and assistants dash about on errands, and at the center of this whirlwind of activity is 12-year-old Dakota Blue Richards, playing Lyra Belacqua. "Here we go!" calls a voice and there is silence, as 50 or more people prepare for filming.

This is scene No. 150, and the setting is nighttime in the Grand Hall of the palace of Ragnar, the King of the Ice Bears. The walls of the lofty studio are covered from ceiling to floor with "greenscreens," which are used so that the backdrop of ice and snow-covered rocks making up the palace's interior can be added digitally at a later date. The floor of old flagstones disappears under drifts of artificial snow and is scattered with fake seal carcasses, gnawed bones, and the skeleton and gigantic skull of a whale. The hall is lit by massive, fiery lanterns, which are suspended on chains from the ceiling.

◄ *At Shepperton Studios, "A" stage (above left) was used to shoot the scenes in the Grand Hall of Ragnar Sturlusson's palace. When computer-generated effects are added, the scene being filmed will closely resemble the original concept art visualization (below left) of Ragnar on his throne.*

► *Dakota Blue Richards – in costume as Lyra Belacqua – prepares to shoot her character's confrontation with the King of the Ice Bears.*

At the far end of the hall there is a raised dais, reached by a series of broad, shallow steps. Ornate hangings, embroidered with a pattern of crowns but now falling into disrepair, flank a huge, cathedral-like window, festooned with icicles and containing dirty, broken panes of glass.

On a great, golden throne sits "Ragnar" — a six-meter-high inflatable Ice Bear who will be replaced on-screen with a computer-generated character when the CGI animators have finished their work. In the meantime, the inflatable bear provides Dakota with something to act with in the scene that is about to be shot. A green Ping-Pong ball on a long stick is raised in front of the throne to give Dakota an "eye-line." This helps her performance by giving her a spot to focus on when she is acting — the ball indicates where the head of the computer-animated Ragnar will be in the final edit of the movie.

An assistant carries out final checks on Dakota's costume — a fur-trimmed, hooded sealskin coat, knitted mittens, a shoulder bag, and fur-topped boots. After a minor adjustment to Dakota's hair and makeup, the young actress takes her place at the far end of the Grand Hall set, ready to approach Ragnar. The First Assistant Director calls out, "Stand by to shoot..." Two cameras are made ready — one on an enormous crane ready to follow Dakota as she walks toward the throne, the other running on rails to cover the shot from one side. The cameramen and soundmen confirm they are ready to go, and the scene is marked with a clapperboard. Everyone waits for the First Assistant Director to give the order to begin..."And ... ACTION!"

◄ *An enormous, ornate throne was created for Ragnar. A giant inflatable bear was positioned on the throne during filming.*

◄ A green Ping-Pong ball on a long pole was used to provide Dakota with an "eye-line" for the position of the yet-to-be-created, computer-animated Ragnar.

Dakota starts walking forward slowly. Now in character as Lyra, she nervously looks around at all the bones and at imaginary, yet-to-be-created CGI bears that will watch her pass. Removing her mittens, Lyra whispers to her dæmon, Pantalaimon (who is in the form of a mouse), to stay hidden. A recording of Pan's voice is played through loudspeakers: "That's fine by me."

"We can beat him, Pan," says Lyra softly as she pushes back the hood of her coat. As Lyra gets closer to the throne, there is a growl and the voice of Ragnar booms out over the studio loudspeakers, demanding: "What is this little thing?" Lyra stops in terror, but manages to curtsy. "Our greetings to you, great king!" she replies in a small voice and then adds, "Or rather, my greetings, not his."

"Not whose?" asks King Ragnar with an angry roar. The camera is now in a tight close-up on Lyra's face as she desperately tries to control her fear and answer the terrifying Ice Bear. "Iorek Byrnison's, Your Majesty," she replies. "What have you to do with Iorek Byrnison?" snarls Ragnar. There then follows a moment of suspended tension before Lyra answers with words that shock and outrage Ragnar: "I am Iorek Byrnison's dæmon." Unable to believe that his old enemy has acquired his own dæmon, the mighty King of the Ice Bears is filled with fury. "How...? HOW...?" There is a second's beat, and then the First Assistant Director calls, "CUT!" Another scene of *The Golden Compass* has been committed to film, or, as they say in the movies, it's now "in the can."

Acting with Greenscreen

Working with greenscreen can be hard work, and Dakota admits that filming such scenes isn't easy. Some of the toughest scenes have been those in which Lyra is talking with Pantalaimon. "I have a green fuzzy sack to represent Pan," says Dakota, "but the trouble is the bond between a child and its dæmon is crucial and it's difficult to feel anything for a green fuzzy sack!" Acting with imaginary characters can also be a difficult process. "It's hard," she says, "to just stand there and say things to a green ball on a stick! But everyone does what they can to help make it seem more real."

Although Dakota has to act with inflatable models and use her imagination during the scenes with King Ragnar, she also gets to work with puppeteer Tommy Luther. Wearing a green bodysuit and special stilts, Tommy provides a human stand-in for the huge Bear-king: "I love it when Tommy is there, walking about on what I call his 'llama legs'! He has a huge bear-head strapped onto his back, and when he stands up he looks so amazingly tall that it gives you a really good idea of what it would actually be like to be that close to one of the bears."

Visual Effects Supervisor Mike Fink agrees. "Tommy is able to move and do things for Dakota, to help her performance, which is important because, unlike a lot of other effects movies, *The Golden Compass* is all about performance. The people on set have to look as though they know what they're looking at and talking to. And if the actors in the film give a really good performance, then our digital actors will look great!"

> *"If the actors in the film give a really good performance, then our digital actors will look great!"*
>
> MIKE FINK

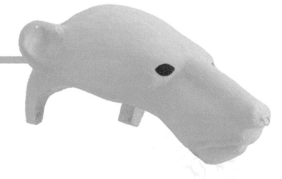

For Dakota, one of the most exciting aspects of working with imaginary costars was riding on the mechanical, moving bear that was specially built for the scenes where Lyra races across the snows of Svalbard on Iorek's back. "That was really fun!" laughs Dakota. "I enjoyed what we called 'the rodeo bear.' The funniest thing was seeing Chris Weitz trying to ride it. He insisted that he needed to know how scary it was if I was going to do it. I was fine on it, but he was sitting there screaming and swearing!"

This meant that the director had to make a contribution to the "swear box" that Dakota started on the set in aid of charity. "Which reminds me," she says, "I think Daniel Craig still owes me around fifty pounds! I really liked Daniel and one of my favorite quotes of his was when I was talking to him about playing James Bond. 'Oh, yeah,' he said, 'that was a good pastime!'"

◄ *Puppeteer Tommy Luther acted as stand-in for King Ragnar on the set of* The Golden Compass.

▶ When Lyra rescues Billy Costa from a trapper's hut in the North, Iorek Byrnison (below) carries them both back to the Gyptian camp. A special machine was built to simulate the motion of the huge Ice Bear running across the snowy landscape. This footage was later combined with computer-generated imagery.

> "It was really helpful to be acting alongside someone as experienced as Nicole Kidman."
>
> DAKOTA BLUE RICHARDS

◀ Dakota enjoyed riding on the mechanical 'rodeo bear' machine during shooting, but for Director Chris Weitz it was a scary experience!

Dakota also enjoyed the opportunity to work with Nicole Kidman, beginning with the very first scene that she filmed for the movie in which she and Mrs. Coulter have dinner in London's Park Lane Hotel. "It was kind of scary meeting her because she's a big star and the strange thing is that although she didn't know me, I felt that I knew her just because I'd seen her movies. But then working with her I really did get to know her and for me, being in front of a camera for the first time, it was really helpful to be acting alongside someone as experienced as Nicole."

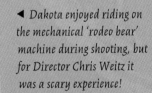

▲ A selection of full-size models and live animals was used during the filming of the movie as "place-markers" to highlight the spaces where CGI dæmons would later be added.

One of the challenges faced by Dakota — and every other actor working on *The Golden Compass* — was the need to be aware that computer-generated dæmons would eventually be sharing many of their scenes on screen. As a result, filming was a constant process of making and refining decisions, as Mike Fink explains:
"The director and I would sit and discuss every shot, deciding whether, for example, he wanted to show Pan as a mouse or whether we needed to reframe the shot so as to give enough room for Pan to be seen as a cat."

The dæmons were particularly tricky in shots where the space on set for them and the characters they belong to was restricted. "When we were going to shoot the characters walking up the ramp to the board the *Noorderlicht*," says Mike, "we had to be absolutely sure that if one of them had a jackal or a warthog for a dæmon, then all of us — including the actor — remembered to keep a decent-sized gap, in front, beside, or behind them or there would be no room later to add in the dæmon."

> "There were 125 kids ... there wasn't a molecule of space left for even a single dæmon — let alone one for each of them."
>
> MIKE FINK

This issue was particularly problematic in the scene in which the children escape from the Experimental Station at Bolvangar. "There were 125 kids," recalls Mike, "and, being kids, they all wanted to be in the movie so they all rushed to the front. And then, secondly, they knew that Dakota was the star, so they all wanted to be around her, which meant that there wasn't a molecule of space left for even a single dæmon — let alone one for each of them!"

◄ Ensuring that the actors left enough space around them for the insertion of CGI dæmons was a constant problem during filming.

For Mike Fink and the rest of the crew, such problems were all in a day's work. "If you do what I do," Mike says, "and you feel totally confident and are sure that you know exactly what you're doing, then you're probably making a big mistake! But if you really feel a little nervous about it, if you're watching everything and you're twitchy all the time — like I've been since I got hired on this film — then you know you're doing the right thing!"

Dæmon Death

One of the most dramatic visual effects in *The Golden Compass* movie is the "dæmon death" sequence. In Philip Pullman's original book, when a human dies, their dæmon simply disappears. In the film, Director Chris Weitz and Production Designer Dennis Gassner decided to create a far more dramatic effect. The early concept art visualization shown above shows the explosive disintegration of a dog-dæmon into a "nebula" of glowing particles. Visual Effects Supervisor Mike Fink and his CGI teams were then given the challenge of creating this stunning effect digitally for the finished movie.

▼ Computer-generated dæmons are a key feature of many scenes in The Golden Compass. It took many months of intensive work by Mike Fink's CGI teams to create Lord Asriel's snow-leopard Stelmaria (left), Lyra's dæmon Pantalaimon (below), and Mrs. Coulter's Golden Monkey (right).

It's a Wrap!

Reviewing the Journey — Editing and Post-Production

It's early March 2007, and the majority of shooting for *The Golden Compass* is complete. However, a vast amount of post-production work still has to be done before the movie is ready to be premiered and released.

Director Chris Weitz has to edit the movie footage, working with veteran film editor Anne V. Coates — who won an Oscar® for editing David Lean's *Lawrence of Arabia* — and Peter Honess, whose pictures have included *Poseidon*, *Æon Flux*, and *Troy*. Peter has received an Academy Award® nomination, and won a BAFTA Award for his editing work on Curtis Hanson's *L.A. Confidential*.

While the film is being edited, Director of Photography, Henry Braham, has to supervise the "color-grading" of the film, a process of adjusting the color balance on every single shot in order to ensure that his concept of a journey of light and color is fully realized in the final version of the movie that is seen on screen.

Then French composer Alexandre Desplat — who has scored, among other films, *Girl With a Pearl Earring*, *Casanova*, *Syriana*, and *The Queen* — will compose the musical score. Sound effects and special acoustics will also be created and added to complete the movie soundtrack.

Though he has still much to do before the release of *The Golden Compass*, it is an opportunity for Chris Weitz to reflect on the project that he fought to get, walked away from and to which he then, miraculously, got the chance to return.

"The second time around," he says, "I was right! I've never regretted it. There's nothing better that I could have been doing. I now know much more than anybody should about making a big effects movie — which is really about making two films at the same time! And because I've had the right people working with me I've been able to get to grips with the huge logistical tasks involved."

◄ *Chris Weitz directs Dakota Blue Richards as they puzzle over the mysteries of the alethiometer during the shooting of the Trollesund scenes.*

▲ Working with actors such as Daniel Craig (above left) and Magda Szubanski (above right) has been an amazing experience for Dakota.

So what were the best moments — the "highs"— of working on *The Golden Compass*? "Well," says Chris, "I've been lucky enough to have one or two 'highs' every single day. Again and again there were times in Dakota's performance when she would get things so right that you couldn't really have imagined that anyone could get there. Perhaps more than anything, those are moments of really deep satisfaction."

For Dakota Blue Richards it is also time to reflect on what it was like to have the opportunity to become Lyra Belacqua. "I had no idea what it was going to be like," she says. "It turned out to be hard work with a lot of early mornings and late nights. I missed my friends and it was odd being with adults the whole time."

Talking frankly, Dakota talks about the ups and downs of the moviemaking process: "Parts of it were boring, especially if I was feeling tired or not too well or if you were shooting a scene that you'd been shooting for the last week, but it was also much more fun than I'd imagined and I didn't think I'd make such close friends with everyone. It was like one big family and I really felt very sad when the time finally came to be going away."

As well as acting in the movie, Dakota had to keep up her school studies, working with an on-set tutor who taught her along with her two doubles, her stunt double, and any other youngsters who were involved in the filming.

"We had to do three hours' school work each day," remembers Dakota, "but there were only ever five of us at most, so it was harder than ordinary school because you had to concentrate more — especially as school was really only in half-hour bursts while they were changing a camera setup around. You'd be trying to learn French verbs and then, suddenly, you'd hear one of the assistants coming along the corridor, shouting into their walkie-talkies, 'OK, I'm pulling her out!'"

There were also occasional disappointments for the actress, including not being allowed to shoot a stunt scene. "I was supposed to shoot the scene where Lyra falls out of Lee Scoresby's airship. They were going to take me up in a harness and then drop me but then they decided to film it with my stunt double instead. Everyone said that they couldn't take the risk because I'd still got two more films to make, but it was the one shot that I was really looking forward to and it wasn't fair!"

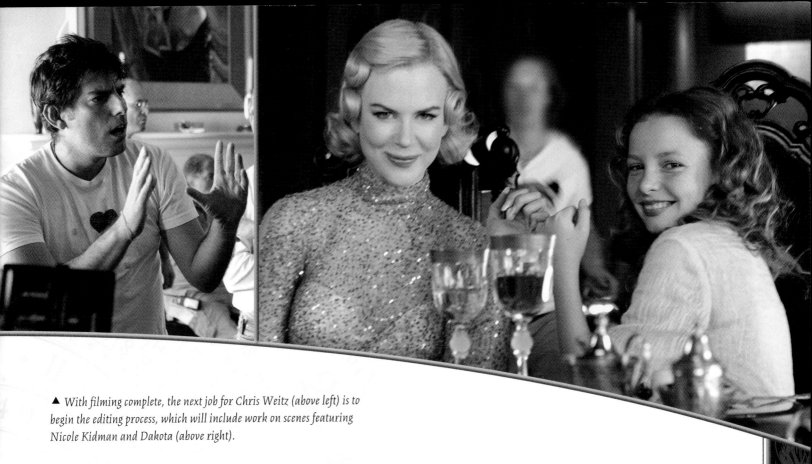

▲ *With filming complete, the next job for Chris Weitz (above left) is to begin the editing process, which will include work on scenes featuring Nicole Kidman and Dakota (above right).*

Talking of Dakota's contribution to the film, Chris Weitz says: "A film set isn't a natural environment and it's really not normal to be working on a film when you're only 12 years old. Dakota had a tremendous amount of responsibility but she was able to handle it and to deliver a really great performance." For Dakota, making *The Golden Compass* has been a life-changing experience. As Director of Photography Henry Braham says: "Dakota has been on a journey and in some ways it's very similar to Lyra's journey in life. There's been a growth and development in her stature as a person just as there is in the character she plays."

Looking back at the end of the shoot, Dakota recalls the first day of filming. "I remember when I first put on Lyra's costume, I looked at myself in the mirror and wasn't really sure who I was looking at. In some ways, it still doesn't feel 100 percent real and I don't think it will until the film comes out. I keep thinking how I felt when I first met Nicole Kidman — as if I knew her when I didn't really — and I think now I might get some of that too because, once the film's released, people will know who I am. To have people come up to you and say, 'Hey, you played Lyra!' That will be really weird!"

When asked if she intends to continue with acting, Dakota thinks for a moment and then says: "When I was younger I wanted to be a teacher or a vet because I thought you might as well think of a job you can do! So many little kids think, 'Oh, I'm going to be a pop star!' and, of course, it never really happens. But, yes, I'd like to go on acting. It would have to be a character that I'd like to play, but maybe it would be best to have another full-time job and just do acting when I really wanted to."

That may not quite be how acting careers work out but, at 12 years old, Dakota is some way off having to make lifelong career decisions. Meanwhile, there are those two other potential movies to be made based on Philip Pullman's *The Subtle Knife* and *The Amber Spyglass*. "I've been having recurring dreams about being on the set of the second and third films," says Dakota. "Sometimes it will only be a quick thing such as somebody shouting 'Action!' but sometimes it will be a whole day in which we're filming scenes from the second or third book. They're only dreams, but I've been having them every single night!"

For Dakota, like Lyra, the journey has just begun....

ACKNOWLEDGMENTS

AUTHOR ACKNOWLEDGMENTS

Telling the behind-the-scenes story of the making of a movie is only possible with the cooperation of the filmmakers, and I am particularly grateful to Deborah Forte, the Producer of *The Golden Compass*. As well as sharing the story of her own long and passionate involvement in bringing *The Golden Compass* to the screen, Deborah also welcomed me onto the set at Shepperton Studios to meet with (in alphabetical order) Henry Braham, Mike Fink, Dennis Gassner, Barry Gibb, Peter King, Ruth Myers, Anna Pinnock, and Chris Weitz. It was also a special privilege to interview Dakota Blue Richards and to hear her talk about both her love of the *His Dark Materials* trilogy and the amazing journey that led to her being cast as Lyra Belacqua. Tom Fickling, Helen Appleby, and Sue D'Arcy provided invaluable help with the setting up of our interviews, for which I am very grateful. Thanks are also due to my friends at *Way With Words*, who undertook the task of painstakingly transcribing many hours of interviews.

I am much indebted to Lisa Edwards, the Editorial Director at Scholastic UK, for having invited me to write this book; to Neil Kelly, Project Manager of Scholastic's *The Golden Compass* publishing program, for his tireless advice, encouragement and friendship, and for his editorial contributions and involvement with many of the interview sessions; to Aja Bongiorno for making my words into such a stunningly designed book; and to Laura Milne for her diligent proofreading. Finally, my personal thanks to my agent, Vivien Green, and my partner, David Weeks, for their support on the journey as the Compass led the way....

SCHOLASTIC UK ACKNOWLEDGMENTS

Scholastic Children's Books would like to thank everyone at Scholastic Media and New Line Cinema for their help in the making of *The Golden Compass – The Official Illustrated Movie Companion*. Special thanks go to Deborah Forte, Chris Weitz, Dennis Gassner, Ruth Myers, Barry Gibbs, Henry Braham, Mike Fink, Peter King, Anna Pinnock, and Dakota Blue Richards for their fascinating and insightful interviews. Thanks also to Tom Fickling and Helen Appleby for their hospitality and invaluable assistance; John Mayo for all his help with picture research and approvals management; Sue D'Arcy and Mickey Richards for facilitating our interview with Dakota; Bapty and Co. Ltd. for supplying items and assisting with our photo shoot at Shepperton Studios; Marion Lloyd and Sarah Lilly for their help researching the Pullman archive; Dereen Taylor for picture research; and, finally, Philip Pullman for his imaginative brilliance in creating the spellbinding worlds of *His Dark Materials* — without which none of this would have been possible.

PICTURE CREDITS

Photography by Laurie Sparham. Additional photography by Michelle Martinoli: Map of the Modern World (pg 9); spirit projector, photogram orbs and case, newspapers, coins, pouch (pg 62); spy-fly and box (pg 63); assorted weapons, Serafina's cloud pine bow, Mrs. Coulter's gun and case (pg 64); Iorek's armor (pg 65); Mrs. Coulter's bureau (pg 66); Lord Asriel's intercision machine (pg 67). Additional credits: Book covers from a selection of different worldwide editions pg 6; Oxford University Press pg 7 (*Paradise Lost* cover); Knopf Publishing Group at Random House pg 8 & pg 12 (*His Dark Materials* jackets); CILIP pg 12 (Carnegie Medal); © Royal National Theatre Enterprises Ltd pg 13 (*His Dark Materials* Theatre Production Programme); Eamonn McCabe, Camera Press London pg 13 (Philip Pullman); © New Line Productions Inc. pg 17 (*Lord of the Rings* trilogy posters).